12/10/19

KT-215-965

THE HAUNTING

For my aunts: Ruth Willrich and Tracy May

STRIPES PUBLISHING
An imprint of Little Tiger Press
1 The Coda Centre, 189 Munster Road,
London SW6 6AW

www.littletiger.co.uk

A paperback original
First published in Great Britain in 2016
Text copyright © Alex Bell, 2016
Cover copyright © Stripes Publishing Ltd, 2016
Photographic images courtesy of www.shutterstock.com

ISBN: 978-1-84715-458-3

Printed and bound in the UK.

10 9 8 7 6 5 4 3 2 1

THE HAUNTING

ALEX BELL

RED EYE

Chapter One

Emma

Here are the first three things I learned about being in a wheelchair:

1. You have to ask for help all the time.
2. You actually have to ask for help *ALL* the time.
3. After a little while, asking for help starts to feel like getting punched in the face.

After the accident, when I was ten, Mum and Dad moved us halfway across the country and refused to speak to Gran. I never blamed her for what happened, and the two of us exchanged letters a few times a year. Then, when I was seventeen, Gran wrote to say she was ill. Seriously ill, dying in fact, and living in a hospice. And she wanted to see me.

I asked Mum if we could go, but she and Gran had never been close, even before the accident. I told my parents that I wanted to see her, even if they didn't – October half-term was about to start so I wouldn't even miss any lessons at college.

"You can't go by yourself, Emma," Mum said.

"I've got the car," I began. "I could—"

"Absolutely not! You passed your test five days ago!"

"Right, I passed it, I didn't *fail* it!"

"You're not doing a six-hour drive alone. You need to get used to the car first."

"What's the point of buying me a specially adapted car if I'm never going to be allowed to drive it?"

But it was no good. I could tell that nothing I said was going to get me anywhere. So I set my alarm for early the next morning when it was still dark outside. Bailey – my lifesaver of a German Shepherd – had been my disability assistance dog for six years, and helped me get washed and dressed like normal. Then he opened the door and carried my bag out to the car. I was terrified the entire time that my parents would hear us, or that some uncanny sixth sense of Mum's would tip her off and she'd come running down the stairs in her pyjamas, flapping her arms and shouting. I wouldn't put it past her to lie down on the road in front of my car like some kind of lunatic. She could be a bit deranged, sometimes, when it came to my safety.

But, with Bailey's help, the whole thing went smoothly and, in no time at all, we were in the car. I buckled Bailey into his doggy safety belt in the passenger seat beside me, and then I was driving away with the biggest sense of achievement. We had done it, we had actually got away with it. I glanced over at Bailey and said, "Road trip time!"

He gazed back at me with his chocolate brown eyes and wagged his tail and I knew that he approved. Bailey approved of everything that I did. If I wanted to do something, he never questioned whether I could or should, he never tried to stop me or warn me – he just helped me do it. No fuss, no doubt, no problem.

Mum had tried to help me before Bailey came along and she never complained about it, not once, but you still feel guilty when you have to ask someone to help you a hundred times a day – whenever you drop something, or can't reach a door, or need to tie your shoelaces, or can't reach a counter in a shop, or can't stand up without wobbling, or need something fetching from upstairs. Bailey knew the words for more than a hundred different objects and he just always seemed so happy whenever I asked him to fetch me something. He'd go running off to get it and then come bounding back to present it to me, tail wagging, brown eyes shining, as if we were playing some kind of game. As if *I* was the one doing *him* the favour.

As I drove down the slip road on to the motorway, I felt a brief flicker of doubt. I'd never even driven on a motorway before. What if Mum was right and I got lost or crashed the car? What if it was weird seeing Gran again after all these years? How could it possibly *not* be weird?

"Shit," I said, my hands gripping the steering wheel.

Maybe this trip was a colossal mistake. Colossal mistakes were kind of my speciality, after all.

But then I felt the soft flick of a warm tongue on my wrist and turned my head to see Bailey looking at me again with that steady brown gaze, so full of trust and belief, as if it never occurred to him even for a moment that I was some helpless invalid who couldn't do anything by themselves. In Bailey's eyes, I was basically Superwoman.

I breathed out and relaxed my grip on the steering wheel. "You're right," I said. "We can do this."

Chapter Two

Emma

After driving for about two hours, Bailey and I stopped for breakfast at a motorway service station.

My parents had been phoning me constantly as soon as they realized I wasn't there. I knew they would be completely freaking out and when I finally answered the phone and told Mum what I was doing, she went mad and even threatened to follow me to Cornwall herself to drag me home.

"Mum, could you please just not make this harder than it already is? I *am* going to see Gran for half-term, and I'm sorry but there's nothing you can do about it."

She sighed. "All right, Emma, if it really means that much to you. But you're not going to stay at … at that place, are you?"

She couldn't even bring herself to say the name.

"The Waterwitch?" I said. It occurred to me then that I hadn't given much thought to where I was actually going to stay. "Um, I guess so. I mean, I won't have to pay for a room there and it's dog-friendly—"

"Stay somewhere else, Emma," Mum said. "Anywhere else. That inn has been nothing but bad luck for our family. Don't worry about the cost – just use that credit card we got you."

I wasn't going to argue with her about it. Going back to the Waterwitch wasn't something I particularly wanted to do after what had happened there last time, and if Mum and Dad wanted to stump up the cash for me to stay somewhere else, then that was fine by me.

"OK, Mum, I will. Thanks. Listen, I have to go – we've got a long way to drive still."

After hanging up, Bailey and I got out of the car and went into the services. Even though he had his green assistance dog jacket on, people would sometimes challenge me about taking him into buildings, but no one did today, and I enjoyed my breakfast in peace.

As we were leaving, a couple of people stopped and asked if they could stroke Bailey, and he looked pleased with himself as they ran their hands down his glossy coat. Bailey adored being the centre of attention. One of the best things about having him with me was that I stopped being the freak in the wheelchair and became instead the girl with the really cool dog.

We continued on our way, stopping again for lunch at another service station. Bailey gave a yelp as he jumped out of the car. It was only a small one, but still, the sound unsettled me. He'd been two years old when he'd come to us so he was eight now, which was getting on a bit for a German Shepherd. I'd noticed him moving stiffly recently and when Mum and I took him to the vet a month ago, she'd said that he was starting to get arthritic. She'd even suggested that it might be time to start thinking about retiring Bailey and getting a new assistance dog. As if we would ever consider packing him off to the organization who had provided him, like some piece of discarded luggage.

"Absolutely not," I'd said. "I don't want another assistance dog; I want Bailey."

"It's just that he might not be able to do all the things you need him to do soon," the vet said.

"I don't need him to do anything other than

be my friend. I don't care if he can't help me any more. I'll get by – I did before. Bailey is part of our family. I won't let him be sent away. He'd think we'd abandoned him."

There was no denying that he was getting older, though. It was just one of those cold little facts that could keep you awake in the middle of the night.

We were making good time until we got stuck in the tailback from an accident further along the motorway. We ended up sitting in it for hours and it was late by the time I turned up at the hospice where Gran was living. The receptionist got a bit snooty with me about visiting hours being almost over but I said, "*Almost* over isn't over, is it? I promise I won't stay long. I just want to let her know that I'm here. Please, I've come a really long way."

She looked at Bailey and I could practically feel her trying to decide whether to kick up a fuss or not. Eventually, she said, "The dog is toilet-trained, right?"

I stared at her. "Are you kidding? He's a qualified disability assistance dog. He probably has a larger vocabulary than you do."

Way to go, Emma, I thought. *Piss off the person in charge. That'll really help the situation.*

The woman gave me a dirty look. Nobody ever expects lip from a person in a wheelchair.

"Could you give me five minutes?" I asked. "Just to say hello?"

Finally the receptionist called someone to take me to Gran. It felt so weird following her down the sterile halls, with their horrible smell of disinfectant mixed with pee and bleach and other things I couldn't identify and didn't really want to think about too much. I just couldn't imagine Gran in a place like this. In my head she was still at the Waterwitch, with its cosy log fires and creaking wooden floors and flickering candles.

We went into a communal living room, where several residents were sitting around in plastic armchairs, watching TV or reading a paper. I didn't recognize Gran at first and, to my shame, the nurse had to point her out to me.

She wasn't the woman I remembered. This was an old, old lady, with bony wrists and an almost skeletal frame. She was sitting at a table with a book in her hand, only she wasn't looking at the book but just staring straight ahead in this listless kind of way that made my stomach clench up in knots.

"Visiting hours are almost over—" the nurse at my side started to say.

"Yes, yes," I waved her into silence. "God, it's like being in prison or something."

Having come all this way, I now didn't know quite what to say or do, and nerves were making me snappy. Suddenly, I felt totally and completely out of my depth. Bailey must have sensed it because he pressed his warm, wet nose into the palm of my hand.

"OK, OK," I said. I buried my fingers in the soft fur at the ruff of his neck for a moment, took a deep breath and then wheeled myself over to where Gran was sitting, my stomach filled with butterflies.

I cleared my throat and said, "Um, hello?"

Gran looked at me with a total lack of recognition. And why shouldn't she? I'd been ten years old the last time she'd seen me. Seven years was a long time. For a gut-wrenching moment, I actually thought I might have to explain who I was.

But then she noticed the wheelchair and I guess it was that she recognized first. She let out this noise somewhere between a shout and a sob. "Oh! Oh, Emma, you came! You came!"

All at once, there were tears in her eyes and she

was struggling up out of her armchair and then awkwardly leaning down to wrap her frail arms around me. God, I hated that I couldn't stand up to hug her back – not without running the risk of falling straight back down on my bum. I was afraid to squeeze her tight like I used to, so I just put my arms around her very gently. I tried to apologize for the number of years that had gone by, while she kept thanking me over and over again for coming, as if I had done something incredible, just by showing up.

Finally, Gran pulled back, and said, "How grown-up you are, Emma! And beautiful, too. I always knew you'd be beautiful."

I flushed, and tried not to squirm with embarrassment. I wasn't beautiful. My mid-length brown hair, green eyes and average size were the definition of ordinary. Gran was just trying to compensate for the wheelchair – the great big metal elephant in the room, the monster in my head, the constant reminder of all that had gone wrong and been broken in our family.

"Where's your mother?" Gran asked. "Just parking the car?"

The hope on her face was painful as she gazed

around, looking for someone who was never coming. I hadn't got round to telling her I'd passed my driving test yet and I guess it never occurred to her that I could get here by myself.

"Gran, she … she didn't come," I said, hating Mum in that moment for refusing even to consider it, and hating myself for not *making* her come somehow. "It's just me."

Gran tried to seem like she didn't mind but I knew that she did, that she minded more than she could say. "Well," she said, sitting back down. "Well. And this must be Bailey?"

She reached out to stroke him and I couldn't stop staring at how gnarled her hands were. The skin covering them was paper-thin.

"He can load and unload the dishwasher," I said, grateful for the fact that Bailey was there because it was easier for us to talk about him than pretty much anything else. "Only Mum won't let him. She says it's unhygienic."

"Can he really? How marvellous," Gran said, rubbing her hand under his chin while Bailey did his best to lick her.

"I don't think they'll let me stay long," I said.

"But I'll come back as soon as I can tomorrow."

"Where are you sleeping tonight?" Gran asked.

"I don't know yet." I glanced at my watch. "I thought I'd have time to sort that out when I arrived, but it took me longer to get here than I thought."

"I hope you weren't thinking of staying at the Waterwitch," Gran said. "Because you can't. I closed it a couple of months ago. It's going to be put up for sale. And I don't want you going there, Emma."

Something about Gran's tone made me curious. "Why not?" I asked.

To my surprise, she reached out and wrapped her bony fingers tightly around my wrist. "The Waterwitch is not a suitable place for you," she said. "It's not a suitable place for any person."

"What do you mean?" I asked, frowning.

It was an old building and I thought Gran would say that there was rot, or damp, or perhaps a particularly vicious mouse problem.

Instead, she looked right at me and said, "The Waterwitch is haunted."

Chapter Three

Emma

My heart sank as I stared at Gran. I could see it there in her eyes: fear. Real-life, actual fear. She honestly believed what she was saying. I could feel her fingers around my wrist trembling slightly. Perhaps her mind had started to wander. She was extremely old now, after all, and ill as well. I was such an idiot for expecting her to still be the same.

"But, Gran," I said gently, "you always used to say that Cornish innkeepers told ghost stories just to drum up business."

"Most of them probably do," Gran replied. "Maybe all of them. I'm not so sure any more. But I do know that the Waterwitch is different. There's a ... a presence there, some malicious presence. Oh, I know how that sounds, I *know*. But if you'd seen what I've seen over the last few months, Emma, you wouldn't doubt it for a moment."

"Well, what *have* you seen?" I asked.

"It doesn't matter now," Gran said, waving my question away. "None of that matters any more. Just promise me you won't set foot in the Waterwitch."

I could see that she was getting upset so I said, "All right, Gran, fine. I promise. Look, I wasn't planning on staying there anyway. Do you know of anywhere nearby that takes dogs?"

"The Seagull will have rooms," Gran replied. "And it takes pets. It's opposite the Waterwitch – do you remember? You'll be OK there."

Just then the nurse came over, saying that visiting time was over and we would have to go.

"Emma, would you do me a favour?" Gran said, as I was about to leave.

"Of course – what is it?"

"Would you drop the keys to the Waterwitch off at the estate agent? It's the one in the high street. I promised I'd post them but, as you're here, perhaps you wouldn't mind? The spare got lost a while ago so we don't want anything happening to this set."

I said I'd be happy to and then waited as Gran shuffled to her room to fetch them. She returned a few minutes later and pressed a ring of keys into my hand. There was one key in particular that stood out from the rest. It was a big black iron thing, cold and heavy in my hand. There was a silver witch key ring attached to it – a proper old hag, with a pointy hat, riding a broomstick. She had warts and everything.

"Just hand the whole lot over," Gran told me. "Some of the smaller keys open other doors inside."

I promised to do as she'd asked and to come back and visit the next day. We said goodbye and then Bailey and I made our way back down the depressing corridor and out into the welcome relief of the cool, fresh air. I wheeled my chair across the car park, Bailey trotting along at my side, and in less than ten minutes, we were driving over the bridge that spanned the river and split the town into East and West Looe. Even in the dark I could see the little boats moored on the water, bobbing gently. There seemed to be large seagulls everywhere I looked, staring at us out of the gloom.

I drove slowly through a narrow street on the edge of the water, behind the shops, where the fish market was. There were even more seagulls there, pecking between the cobbles in search of fish guts and scraps. The shutters of the market were pulled down but that didn't stop the entire street from reeking of fish

– I could smell it even from inside the car.

By the time we reached the quayside the smell had been replaced with salted air, seaweed and fresh paint. Strings of white lights reflected off the dark water and the fishing boats moored there. They bumped against their wooden posts as we drove past, in rhythm with the lapping of the water. I saw hand-painted signs advertising boat trips and a ferry service that would take you across to the other side of the river for only a few pence. When I was a kid I used to do that all the time with my best friend, Jem Penhale. We'd go across to visit our favourite sweet shop and spend the last of our pocket money. Or, at least, I would spend my pocket money. Jem's dad didn't give him pocket money so I would buy sweets for both of us and he would pay me back by finding pink shells along the beach afterwards.

It was all so familiar. I had expected it to be different somehow. Even Banjo Pier looked just the same, stretching out into the dark ocean. Jem and I had spent hours there on sunny summer days, watching the sea and the ships and the swooping seagulls. I hoped that I wouldn't see him while I was here. It would just be so awkward. We'd been best friends once, but I'd have no idea what to say to him now. After my accident, Jem had tried to visit me in hospital, but I didn't want to see anyone then, not even Jem, so I'd told Mum to send him away. When she came back into my hospital room she'd pressed a small bronze charm into my hand and said, "Jem asked me to give you this."

It was Joan the Wad, the Queen of the Piskies. Legend had it that she led travellers astray on the Cornish moors, but if you kept a good luck charm of her about your person then she would light your way home instead.

Good fortune will nod if you carry upon you Joan the Wad.

I recognized the charm because I had bought it myself, a couple of years before, at the Joan the Wad and Piskey Shop in Polperro, as a gift for Jem after his mother died.

"He said to say that you need her more now," Mum said, as I stared down at the tiny bronze figure.

I put the charm on a silver chain to wear as a necklace and had worn it every day since, like some kind of talisman. I could feel the weight of it now, reassuring beneath my shirt. We moved soon after that and I never saw Jem again. I thought about writing to him when I first wrote to Gran but what would I say? And now, seven years had gone by and we didn't know each other any more.

My stomach clenched in a familiar ache of longing for a life that could never be again so I tried to think about something else, anything else really, and, in another couple of minutes, my car was parked on the cobbles outside the Seagull. I looked across the road at the Waterwitch. The old building was all dark slate and stone, thick bottle-glass windows and leaning, crooked angles. I stared up at the façade and it seemed unnatural to see it without wood smoke curling from the chimneys and orange lights glowing in the windows. Hunched there in the gloom it looked like a dead old shell of a thing.

The sign hung out over the pavement, creaking on rusty hinges in the breeze. I'd forgotten that sign but it came back to me now. There was a picture of the *Waterwitch* ship after it had sunk. You could tell it was a sunken boat because of the barnacles clinging to the prow, the shredded sails, and the algae covering the portholes and coating the anchor. It was a sad, ruined sight.

I put down the ramp and wheeled out my chair. Bailey hopped out of the car and took my bag from the boot, all set to carry it like he'd been trained to, but I could still hear that yelp replaying in my head from earlier so I took the bag from him and set it on my lap instead.

"Thanks, Bailey," I said, patting his head. "But I'll carry it this time."

We went into the Seagull and I checked in. Log fires made it cheerful and homely, and I was soon settled in a pleasant ground-floor room that looked out on to the street and the Waterwitch opposite. Even though it held awful memories for me as well as good ones, I was still sorry to see the Waterwitch all shut up and empty like that. I couldn't believe Gran actually thought it was haunted. She'd always been so dismissive of that kind of thing before, and had scorned those Cornish pubs that banged on about their supposed ghosts – like the Jamaica Inn on Bodmin Moor, or the Dolphin Tavern at Penzance, or the Crumplehorn Inn at Polperro.

I gave Bailey his dinner, ate the sandwich that had been sent to my room and then called home to let my parents know I'd arrived and had somewhere to stay. Once I hung up, Bailey helped me to change into my pyjamas, and I was in bed shortly after 9 p.m. – which was pretty early for me, but all the driving and worrying and remembering had thoroughly worn me out. I fell asleep almost at once and didn't wake up until just gone midnight when I had to get up to go to the loo.

That's a two-minute job for most people. Not so for me. Even with Bailey's help it took forever. As soon as I switched on the lamp, Bailey was there in front of me, my walking stick in his mouth. I took it from him and, as I struggled to my feet, he moved around to put his large body behind me, helping to steady me. Then began the slow process of shuffling towards the bathroom.

Finally, I got there, used the loo and then began the journey back to my bed. I stopped by the window to catch my breath for a moment, and, as I stood there, preparing to take my next step, I happened to glance at the Waterwitch across the dark street. The black windows were like eyes staring back at me, and I could see the sign still swaying gently back and forth in the soft light from a nearby lamp post. And then, all of a sudden, I saw it – the smallest flicker of light from one of the first floor windows, like the glow from the flame of a candle. It wasn't stationary, but moving, as if someone was holding the candle and walking across the room with it.

In a matter of seconds, the light passed out of sight and, although I watched for several minutes, it didn't reappear in any of the other windows. I blinked and rubbed at my eyes. Gran had said that the Waterwitch was closed, hadn't she? Perhaps someone had broken in and was squatting there?

I turned away from the window, told myself I'd think about it in the morning, and continued on back to bed. My back throbbed as if I'd just run a marathon – with a gigantic cow strapped to my back. I reached over for the painkillers I always kept within reach and knocked back a couple. It would be a little while before they took effect, though, and I was tense as I lay there, waiting for it to ease.

Bailey always knew when I was in pain and hopped on to the bed beside me to curl up against my back. The heat from his body helped ease the ache a little and I knew I'd have a much better chance of getting back to sleep with Bailey snuggled up beside me.

"It doesn't hurt," I told myself firmly. "It doesn't hurt at all."

Chapter Four

Emma

I got up early the next morning and went through my usual routine with Bailey. He fetched my clothes and helped me get dressed and into the wheelchair, and then we made our way to the restaurant.

Visiting hours at Gran's hospice didn't start till the afternoon, meaning I had a bit of time to kill after breakfast. I was very aware of the chunky weight of the Waterwitch keys in my bag. Perhaps I'd imagined that light last night, or it had just been a street lamp reflecting in the thick glass, but if there was someone squatting in the Waterwitch then Gran would have to know. I decided to go over the road and check it out, only feeling a twinge of guilt about breaking my promise to her because, really, the whole thing was daft.

I put on my coat and helped Bailey into his jacket, then we headed out and across the cobbled street to the Waterwitch. The lock clicked easily and I told Bailey to open the door as I dropped the keys back in my bag.

Only Bailey didn't move. I turned in surprise and saw that he was standing on the pavement, his ears pricked up, just staring at the door.

"Bailey," I said again. "Open."

I thought maybe he hadn't heard me the first time, but he ignored the second command, too. Bailey was such a well-trained, obedient dog. He *never* ignored me like this. And then, to my complete astonishment, he growled – a deep, rumbling growl right at the back of his throat. His lips pulled back, exposing his long white canines.

"Hey!" I said sharply. "Bailey, no!"

He stopped straight away and had the grace to look a little ashamed of himself. Then he decided to obey me after all and pushed the door open with his front legs. But his behaviour had made me uneasy. I'd never seen him act like that and the thought flashed across my mind that perhaps I should lock the place back up and hand the keys over to the estate agent like I'd promised. They could check for squatters themselves. Now that I was right here on the doorstep, though, I felt a strong urge to see the inn again for myself. Maybe it was nostalgia for the past, maybe it was the morbid desire to poke at an old wound but, either way, surely it couldn't hurt to just have a quick look around?

"Good boy," I said to Bailey, scratching him behind the ear as I wheeled myself over the threshold. The main door led straight into the restaurant and, for just a moment, I saw people sitting at the tables, all looking at me, all waiting for me to say something. Then the illusion was gone and I was looking at a dark, empty restaurant. Just an ordinary room filled with the chilly bareness of a place that had been left shut up for too long.

Behind me, Bailey whined and I twisted around to see that he was standing in the doorway, staring at me, an uncertain look in his intelligent brown eyes.

"Come on, silly." I clicked my fingers. "We haven't got all day."

He hesitated a moment but then he walked through – or slunk through, anyway, with his tail between his legs – and nosed the door closed behind him. The restaurant wasn't a sunny room, even during the day. The low ceiling and the dark wood panelling made it a dim space, but I could see that it looked just as I remembered, and everything had been left as it was with even the tables neatly covered in their white tablecloths. There was no mess or litter, no sign of any squatters.

The sloping boards creaked as I wheeled over to the cold fireplace. A huge jar of fish hooks stood on the mantelpiece – gleaming, monstrous things with sharp, cruel barbs. Looking at them was like looking at a jar full of shark's teeth. The two Cornish luck stones were still there, set into the wall beside the hearth, and I ran my fingers over them lightly, just like I used to when I was a kid.

A model of the *Waterwitch* ship sat next to the fish hooks, trapped inside its dusty glass bottle, and it seemed like no time at all had passed since I'd stood here with Gran as she told me the story of the ghost ship.

There were old placards hung on the wall, explaining the history, and I scanned over them to remind myself. The *Waterwitch* had been built at the Royal Dockyard at Deptford in 1577 by a company owned by a wealthy Cornish gentleman from Looe named Christian Slade. When I was a kid there'd been a reproduced painting of him in the restaurant but it wasn't there any more. It must have been taken away fairly recently, though, because I could see a slightly less faded patch on the wall, marking the place where it had been. I wondered what had happened to it.

I turned my attention back to the placards and read that the *Waterwitch*, once finished, had been a 140-foot long, three-masted, 400-ton-galleon. Things started to go wrong before it even left the docks, starting with Christian Slade himself. Shortly before work began on the ship, Christian had accused a village woman of witchcraft and she had been put to death. Because of this, he was fearfully paranoid about being cursed or ill-wished, and had given orders for the ship to have a witch bottle built into the prow for protection. I couldn't help shuddering when I read this part – I already knew all about Christian Slade and his witch bottle.

"It's a type of concealed charm," Gran had told me when I asked about it all those years ago. *"To provide protection against witches. People used to hide them under the floorboards or behind the fireplace. If the bottle was ever found or broken then they thought they'd have no protection against the witch who'd cursed them."*

She went on to tell me about how Christian Slade

had visited the dockyard to inspect the work being done on the ship and was furious to discover that the witch bottle hadn't been put on board yet. And, even worse, the ship had incorrectly been named the *Waterwitch*. No one would admit to having painted the name on the prow but Christian believed someone had done it to mock his fear of witches, and threatened to have all the workers flogged. He became inexplicably enraged when he saw the ship's figurehead and was in the middle of a heated argument with the overseer about it when a huge wooden beam that was being moved fell from its ropes and landed right on top of him, crushing his chest. His lungs collapsed, his ribs were broken and one of them pierced straight through his heart. It took ten men to lift the beam off him, and, by that time, Christian had suffered an agonizing death right there on deck.

Gran told me that everyone got all worked up about the *Waterwitch* after that because, in the sixteenth century, it was considered really unlucky for a man to die on a ship before it had even left port. I looked at the final placard and read that, after a few years of troublesome voyages, the *Waterwitch* set out on its last-ever journey and promptly vanished. Everyone assumed it must have sunk, or been attacked by pirates, but, two years later, it was discovered by a fishing boat, drifting aimlessly in the mist off the south-east coast of Cornwall with not a soul on board. Every single one of the two-hundred-and-sixty-man crew had simply disappeared without a trace. There was no sign of a disturbance or fight, and the lifeboats were all accounted for.

After discovering the *Waterwitch* they attempted to tow it back to harbour but it sank in the storm that followed. Shortly after that, the wood was salvaged from the seabed and used to construct the Waterwitch Inn. I remembered Gran telling me that that was how the guest house had got its name – and the reason why there were so many paintings and models of the ship around.

The timber had legally belonged to one of Christian Slade's relatives and the inn had stayed in the same family for generations, going right down to Jem's mother. But then they fell on hard times and Jem's parents sold the place to Gran shortly before my accident. I glanced back at the faded rectangle on the wall, where the painting of Christian Slade used to be, and remembered how Jem had always jokingly referred to it as "*Grandpa's gloomy old portrait*".

There were lots of paintings of the *Waterwitch* ship still displayed on the walls and it looked just like one of those galleons you saw on old-fashioned maps. The most impressive painting of all was a gigantic oil one that hung over the fireplace. When I was a kid I had always been a little afraid of it.

The ship was depicted in the middle of a stormy sea, the silvery light of the moon shining white on the black foaming water that churned all around. The figurehead was a woman with a white dress and long black hair. At first glance, she seemed beautiful, but when you looked closer there was something almost a bit mad about her expression. Her eyes were too big and vacant, and they were set just a little too far apart on her face. And her lips were drawn back in a way that made it hard to tell whether she was smiling or grimacing – almost as if she could feel the freezing foam and salted sea spray that kept slamming into her wooden body over and over again.

The ship was poised right at the crest of a monstrous wave that had just reached its zenith and looked like it was about to come crashing back down with a vengeance. You could almost hear the shattering of splintered wood, and the ripping of great sails torn from groaning masts.

I was so focused on the ship itself that I didn't notice the birds at first but I remembered them as soon as I saw them again. They were flying all around, flitting like bats between the sails and the rigging and the water. They were entirely black – except for one white spot, just above the tail.

Even now that I was older, I still felt there was something odd about that painting. I stared up at it for quite a long time, trying to work out what it was about those glistening dark oil strokes that bothered me, but I just couldn't put my finger on it.

I turned away and looked at the sea of tables, remembering how I used to play hide-and-seek in the restaurant with Jem and his sister, Shell. With all its nooks and crannies, the Waterwitch had always been a great place for hide-and-seek but the thought of those games now made regret twist unbearably in my stomach.

The three of us should never have gone down to the cellar. Gran had made it clear that we weren't allowed in there, and that it was dangerous while the builders were working. But the huge granite fireplace had seemed like such a great place to hide, especially with all that scaffolding around it.

The cellar was lit by one bare light bulb and the room was covered in sheets that reminded me of sails, even though they were streaked with dirt. They were laid on the floor and walls, and all around the big old stone fireplace in the corner. The builders must have been working on this because some of the stone bricks were in a pile on the floor, and bits of the fireplace were held up with supports. It was the perfect hiding place — until Jem followed me there.

"Find your own hiding place!" I grumbled. "You're going to give us away."

"There's plenty of room for both of us," he replied, ignoring my protests and squeezing in beside me.

"Ouch! Quit sticking your elbow into my face!"

"Why don't you move back a bit?"

"I don't want to get my clothes dirty."

The sound of our argument soon brought Jem's seven-year-old sister, Shell, down to the cellar.

"I could hear you from the top of the stairs," she said,

crouching down to peer through the scaffolding at us. "Don't you know you're supposed to be quiet when it's your turn to hide?"

"I told you you were going to ruin it," I said, giving Jem a shove. He knocked into one of the supports and a cloud of dust rained down on us both.

"Ew, gross!" I cried. "Are there any spiders in my hair?"

"Loads of them," Jem said helpfully. "Nasty little red ones. They look like biters."

He grinned at me and that was when I saw it over his shoulder – the green glint of glass from behind the brick hearth, winking out at me like a giant goblin's eye.

"What's that?" I said.

"What?"

"There's something hidden behind the wall."

"Maybe you should come out of there," Shell said nervously. "Mum always used to say that fireplaces were dangerous because they led to the sky and evil spirits could come down into the house and take you away. She said that—"

"Mum said a lot of stuff that never made any sense," Jem replied, before reaching his hand through the gap and trying to pull out the object. "It's stuck."

I peered over his shoulder to get a closer look.

"It's a bottle, I think," he said, and I heard the clink of

glass as he tried to squeeze it through the gap in the bricks.

"Maybe it's got a secret message inside it!" I said, thrilled at the thought.

"From pirates?" Jem asked eagerly.

"No, from a mermaid."

"Don't touch it!" Shell cried. "Don't disturb it, Jem, it's got something to do with witches."

Jem rolled his eyes. "First it's evil spirits and now it's witches. Make up your mind, Shell. You'll be worried about Santa Claus coming down the chimney next."

"It's a witch bottle," she insisted. "I saw a picture in one of Mum's books. It's got something bad trapped in it. The book said people used to hide them behind fireplaces in the olden days to protect themselves. Not from good witches, like Mum and me, but bad ones who wanted to curse them and—"

"It's almost there," Jem said, ignoring her. Shell had been going on about witches and witchcraft even more since their mum had died a couple of years ago, and we had both long since lost interest in the subject.

"Let me do it," I said, pushing Jem out of the way. "I've got smaller hands than you."

I reached my hand through the gap, gripped the cold neck of the bottle and tugged. There was a shattering sound as it came through, and a piece of it broke off, slicing my palm.

"Ouch!" I cried, dropping the bottle on the ground between us.

Then there was a blast of wind — a blast strong enough to blow the hair back from our faces and whirl the dust up into clouds that made us sneeze — and it seemed to come straight from the bottle on the floor.

"Jem Penhale," Shell said on the other side of the scaffolding, sounding strange and unlike herself. "Seven more years."

"What?" Jem peered through the supports at his sister and said, "What are you talking about?"

She gave him a startled look. "I wasn't the one speaking."

"Yes, you were." Jem sighed. "I don't know why you always have to lie all the time."

"I've never lied to you, ever!"

It was an old argument and I didn't want them falling out, so I quickly changed the subject. "It felt like something came out of the bottle."

"It must have been a draught from the chimney," Jem said. "Is your hand OK, Emma?"

"Yeah, it's OK," I replied. I wiped the blood off on my trousers and then picked up the bottle, which made a clinking sound as I lifted it. "There's something inside," I said.

The bottle was made from green glass that was cracked and old. It had a fat body and a thin neck.

"Hey, look, there's a face on it," Jem said, pointing at the neck of the bottle.

It was no ordinary face. In fact, it wasn't human at all. It was a snarling devil's face, with bulbous, staring eyes, wild eyebrows and a twisting, angry mouth. The cork in the top of the bottle had been sealed with black wax that trickled down the neck in fat dribbles.

I tilted the bottle and shook it to get at the objects that had been concealed inside. Sand poured out on to the floor, followed by several bent, rusty nails; a collection of broken seashells; tiny yellowed bones that looked like they'd come from a small animal, and a piece of plaited human hair.

"Gross!" I wrinkled my nose.

Jem prodded the plait with his fingertip. "Cool."

"There's something else still in there," I said, giving the bottle a final shake.

A thin scroll of ancient yellowed paper fell out and landed on top of the pile. I snatched it up eagerly, excited to discover that there was a message hidden inside the bottle after all. But it was only two sentences long, and definitely wasn't from mermaids.

This bottle was made at the request of the owners of the inn, and entraps the witch that cursed Christian Slade and the Waterwitch ship. If you are reading this note then may God have mercy on your soul.

I looked up at the others. Jem was frowning and Shell looked like she was about to cry. Her voice was almost a whisper as she said, "It's really, really, really bad luck to break a witch bottle, Emma."

"Shell, don't tell Dad about this, OK?" Jem said quickly. "You know he hates witchcraft stuff."

"We'd better not tell Gran, either," I said, gathering up the objects and stuffing them back in the bottle. "She said we're not supposed to be down here while the builders are around."

"Let's get out of here," Jem said.

He was already scrambling out of the fireplace and, in another moment, was on the other side of the scaffolding. I shoved the bottle right to the back of the hearth and made to follow him. But then my foot knocked against one of the supports and, this time, more than dust came down. The sound was deafeningly loud in the small space as the bricks rained all around me. I could hear Jem shouting at me to get out but it was too late. The rest of the fireplace collapsed *and, moments later, my back went strange and tingly, like cold hands clamped all the way along my spine. Cold hands — that's what it feels like when your spine breaks in three different places. It's not a feeling that you ever forget...*

Chapter Five

Emma

My thoughts were torn away from the past when I heard a sound from the floor above. A creaking noise, like footsteps. Bailey heard it, too, looked up at the ceiling and immediately started to growl again. Perhaps there was a squatter here, after all?

I wheeled myself across the restaurant to the opposite door. I didn't want to go through because the door leading down to the cellar was out there and I felt a kind of horror at the thought of seeing it again – the place where it had all happened. No more normal for me after that, not ever. The witch bottle had been completely destroyed in the accident and I was glad because I never wanted to lay eyes on that horrible old thing again. But the staircase that led to the first floor was out there so I gave Bailey the command and, this time, he opened the door straight away and we went through to the shadowy corridor beyond.

I kept my eyes firmly turned away from the cellar door and made straight for the staircase that led up to the guest rooms. It was made from wood so dark that it looked almost black, and into it had been carved the most intricate sea creatures. Jem, Shell and I always used to call it the Monster Staircase when we were small. A sea monster was one of the more dramatic theories for what might have happened to the vanished crew of the *Waterwitch*. The idea was that they had been attacked by some creature from the deep that had devoured them all, although how it managed to do this without sinking the entire ship, or at least damaging it, was something no one could really explain.

Carved into the wood of the staircase were giant squids, sharks, whales, octopuses, kraken, serpents, sea spiders, underwater wasps and other creatures I couldn't even identify – things with spiny barbs along their backs, or gaping gills in their flabby necks, or two heads rising up from bloated bodies. Awful, twisted monsters straight out of a feverish, crazy nightmare.

Eyeballs stared out at me in the gloom from a mass of tails and tentacles, fins and fangs, suckers and scales. I had a vague memory that there were mermaids and sirens at the top of the staircase, but it was too dark for me to see them up there. The balustrades were encrusted with carvings of barnacles, seaweed and shells, like they were trying to trick you into believing you were at the bottom of the sea. That you had gone down with the ship. That this was some hideous afterlife you would never escape from.

I wheeled myself forward until my wheels bumped against the bottom step with a thump.

The Waterwitch was far too old a building to be properly accessible for disabled people. There were no ramps here, let alone lifts. I peered up the staircase, stretching away into the dusty gloom of the silent floor above.

"Hello?" I called out.

Nothing answered me, which wasn't all that surprising. Either there was no one here or there was someone who wasn't supposed to be, in which case they were hardly going to answer. God, I hated this stupid wheelchair! If only I could run up those stairs and check the rooms out for myself. The nearby squid carved into the bannister seemed like it was looking at me with its single, staring eye, mocking me for being trapped in the chair.

I would just have to tell the estate agent about my squatter theory and let them handle it. With one last glance at the dark staircase, I turned my wheelchair around, intending to go back to the restaurant.

But then there was the soft, soft shriek of creaking hinges in the darkness and, right in front of me, the door leading down to the cellar swung slowly open, gaping wide like a monstrous mouth that sought to swallow me up, wheelchair and all. Inch by inch, the door came all the way open until it hit the wall with a faint, gentle thud. I swallowed hard, staring at that dark rectangle, remembering the crash from years ago, the reverberation shuddering through my bones. I told myself it was just a door, that this was an old building, and there must be draughts…

I wheeled myself slowly forwards, past the silent, watching eyes of the carved sea monsters, the weight of my chair causing the wooden floorboards beneath to creak out their protest. The thought flashed loud and clear in my mind that the Waterwitch Inn didn't want me here, didn't want anyone here, only wanted to be left alone in its solitude, like an oyster entombed in its shell. It was a cold feeling of hostility that I sensed out of nowhere, a feeling that told me I wasn't welcome and should leave at once.

I shook my head firmly. Doors swung open by themselves sometimes. It didn't mean anything. That long draughty staircase leading down to the cellar was bound to act like a kind of wind tunnel. Or perhaps the ancient wood in the building had started to shrink or expand or rot or whatever it was that ancient old wood did when it was more than four hundred years old. There could be woodworm or shipworm. Or perhaps the wood had warped.

Even from a little distance away, I could see that the entire door leading down to the cellar was made out of wooden planks. They were long and thin and pocked with ugly black knots, like the scars left by some kind of pox.

I would have ignored the door and gone straight back to the restaurant if it hadn't been for Bailey, but he trotted over in his typically curious way, always wanting to poke his snout into everything.

When he reached the doorway he froze, his entire body completely rigid, his hackles raised, and then he was barking like I had never heard him bark before. A frantic, ferocious sound that was almost a howl, with both his wolf's ears pressed back flat against his head.

"Bailey," I said. "Stop it."

But I doubt he even heard me over the awful din he was making. I moved my chair forwards and the stairs leading down to the cellar came into view. I shuddered at the sight of them. Surely it was just the memory of what had happened last time I was there, not helped by Bailey's reaction, but I suddenly had the strongest sensation that there was something down there and that it was *looking* at us, looking at us from out of that dark, damp room, with eyes wide and teeth bared as if warning us not to come another step closer.

I flung out my arm and slammed the door closed, making the wood shake and shudder in its hinges. I was breathing hard and my hands were trembling slightly. I definitely didn't want to be in the Waterwitch any more. Bailey stopped barking and turned to open the door that led back to the restaurant without my even having to tell him to. I wheeled through it quickly, glad to leave that awful door behind us.

I couldn't help glancing back as I passed through to the restaurant and, in that moment, the wooden planks of the door looked changed somehow. Twisted up into unnatural shapes that hurt my eyes and hurt my head and made me want to get as far away from there as possible. The wood looked knotted up in all the wrong directions, curling around and around on itself like angry waves in a stormy sea, only the angles were all wrong, and just looking at them seemed to do something to my brain, put pressure on some blood vessel behind my eyes somewhere that felt like it might burst at any moment...

I blinked quickly and, when I opened my eyes, the door looked normal once again, almost taunting me with how completely ordinary it was. I told myself that it must have been some trick of the light – and then Bailey nosed the door closed and cut it off from my view.

"Come on," I said. "Let's get out of here."

Bailey didn't need telling twice. He trotted ahead of me to the door that led back to the street but, just as he lifted his paw to pull down the handle, there was a quiet, dreadful click – the unmistakeable sound of the lock turning. It was the softest of noises but I don't think I could have been more shocked if a cannon had gone off behind my head. The lunatic thought occurred to me that the Waterwitch was trying to prevent us from leaving, and my knuckles were white as I gripped the door handle and pulled down on it. Bailey jumped up to press his front paws against the door but it didn't budge. We were definitely locked in.

I balled my hand into a fist and slammed it hard against the wood. "Hey!" I shouted. I don't know who I thought I was shouting at but, the next moment, the lock clicked back and the door was suddenly thrown open. I hadn't realized quite how dark it was inside the Waterwitch until the bright sunlight made me blink and squint like some troll that had been living in an underground cave for   the past year.

Someone stood silhouetted in the doorway before us, someone tall and slim, and then a voice spoke, a single word that was an exclamation of pure, complete surprise: "*Emma?*"

I raised my hand and squinted at him. "I'm sorry, do I—?"

"It's Jem. Jem Penhale."

Chapter Six

Emma

For a few moments, we were both speechless. It was so weird seeing Jem as a teenager. I guess in my head he was still ten, not this tall seventeen-year-old wearing jeans and a black jacket. He was still slender, although perhaps not quite as gangly as he'd been before, and his hair was the usual mess, as if he'd only just got out of bed. But his eyes had changed, or, at least, the left one had. It was no longer the chocolate brown I remembered but sea-green instead. And he looked tired – painfully, obviously tired – with dark bags under his eyes and a sort of pale-skinned, hollow-cheeked look.

"*What happened to you?*" I wanted to say. "*What's wrong? Tell me what I can do to fix it.*"

But I managed to check myself in time. He'd probably just been out clubbing last night. That was what most teenagers did on a Friday night, wasn't it? It was what a lot of my friends did. It's not so easy going clubbing if you're in a wheelchair, though. I tried it once and people kept sitting down in my lap.

"Your eye—" I blurted like an idiot.

Jem stared back. "You... You're in a ... a—"

"Wheelchair?" I gave him the word, trying to be kind. Most people seemed uncomfortable saying it around me, for some reason – as if perhaps I might not have noticed I was actually in a wheelchair at all and that the mere speaking of the word in my presence might make me suddenly look down and say, "Right, stop everything! What is *this*?"

So I said the word to spare Jem from having to say it himself, but my voice came out far more bitter than I'd meant it to, and the word ended up sounding more like a weapon.

Jem flinched. "No one told me," he said. "When I asked your gran about you, she said you were fine."

I wondered if she'd been trying to protect my privacy or something but I couldn't help wishing that she'd just told Jem the truth. It would have made this conversation a lot easier if he'd known what to expect.

"Who's this?" he asked, crouching down in front of Bailey, who instantly offered him his paw.

"That's Bailey," I said. "He's my assistance dog."

Jem was close enough that I could see the chestnut glints in his hair and the unfamiliar green flecks in his left eye.

"So what happened to your eye then?" I asked.

"Oh." Jem paused. "Sometimes when you injure your eye it can change colour, apparently." He shrugged, like it was no big deal.

I wanted to ask if his father had punched him, but I didn't. That was the kind of blunt enquiry I could have made when we were best friends but it really wasn't the kind of thing you could just come out with to someone you hadn't seen in seven years. His dad had given him a black eye. We both knew it. It would have been cruel to make him say it out loud.

I thought of that day hiding away from everyone in the school cupboard when Jem had sobbed quietly in the dark and I'd pressed the Joan the Wad charm into his hand and told him I would always be his friend. It seemed like a long, long time ago now, and the thought of that day made me feel sad, made all my other friendships back home seem kind of feeble and false.

As if reading my mind, Jem stood up and said, "Cool necklace."

My hand went to it instinctively. Perhaps I ought to take this moment to apologize for refusing to see him when he'd tried to visit me in the hospital, but I really didn't want to talk about that day or what had happened.

"Do you always wear it?" Jem asked.

"Um, yes, most days." I suddenly felt embarrassed about it and tucked the charm back under my top, then cleared my throat and said, "I thought I heard footsteps from the first floor just a moment ago." I gestured over my shoulder at the Waterwitch. "Do you think there might be——?"

"That was me," Jem said at once. "I was just inside, checking the rooms upstairs. I came down through the back entrance. We must have just missed each other."

I frowned. "But ... what were you doing in there?"

"Your gran made me the caretaker," Jem replied. He held up a bunch of keys and I saw they were an exact replica of my own. "When she decided to close down the inn and put it up for sale. I used to work in the restaurant here but now I come in a couple of times a week just to check the place and keep it clean."

"Oh. Gran never said. But last night I thought I saw a light in one of the windows. From my room." I gestured at the Seagull across the street. "It was the middle of the night."

"Perhaps it was just a reflection from a street lamp," Jem said. "Is that when you arrived? Last night?"

"Yes."

"How long will you be staying?"

"I'm not sure yet. A week? I came to see Gran because, you know, her health…"

Jem nodded. "Are your parents with you?"

"No. They wouldn't come. I came by myself. With Bailey."

I didn't really want to talk about the mess that was my family life so I said, "How's Shell? She must be, what, fourteen now?"

"She's OK."

"Does she still think she's a witch?"

Jem grimaced and I knew that meant yes.

"Well," he said, "if you're going to be here for half-term then perhaps we could go and get some fish and chips or something? If you want to, I mean."

"Yeah. That would be nice." I hated how stiff and awkward my voice sounded.

I scribbled down my number, thrust the piece of paper at him and then made some bizarre excuse about having to go and comb Bailey's fur.

"Sure, OK," Jem said with a quizzical look. "I work in the restaurant at the Seagull, actually, so I'm sure I'll see you around. Let me know when you want to get those fish and chips." He smiled then and added, "My treat for all those sweets you used to buy me."

The smile made him look more like the boy I used to know and I felt myself relax just a fraction. "I will," I said.

Jem pointed at the Waterwitch and said, "I'm going back in for a moment. I just realized there's something I forgot to do."

"OK. By the way, there's something wrong with the cellar door," I said. "It swung open by itself when I was in there before."

Jem went suddenly rigid, and then turned slowly back round to face me. "The cellar door?" he asked.

"Yeah. I think the wood's warped."

He was frowning. "The *cellar* door was open?"

"Yes." I looked at him, puzzled by his reaction.

There was such an odd expression on his face that I wondered whether perhaps he didn't like me mentioning such a thing to him – as if he were the hired help, only useful for patching up dodgy doors. Perhaps I should have stuck to the dog grooming line of conversation.

"I'll take a look," he said eventually. "Thanks."

I'd definitely offended him. I shouldn't have mentioned the door at all. What was wrong with me? I might just as well have told him that the toilets needed unblocking and the rat traps needed de-goring.

Way to go, Emma, I thought to myself. *You have managed to make a total mess of this conversation. Congratulations. You are an idiot.*

"I'll text you later," I promised, trying my best to sound like a friend and not like someone's boss.

Jem gave me another quick smile. "I'd like that."

I felt the sudden, almost overpowering urge to touch him – just to check that he was definitely there and OK and real. Something about that hollow look he had bothered me. Before I knew what I was doing, my hand was reaching out and I was resting my fingers against the sleeve of his jacket.

"Hey, Jem?" I said. "Are you OK? I mean, really?"

He twisted his arm and, at first, with a flash of hurt, I thought he was trying to pull away from me. Instead, he brought his hand up to mine and wrapped his fingers around my palm. I'd forgotten how warm Jem's hands always were. A memory came back to me suddenly of watching the seafront fireworks display on New Year's Eve when we were kids and making Jem hold my hands because they were cold. That was before the accident, before the wheelchair, before everything changed.

Jem squeezed my fingers briefly before letting them go. "Never better," he said, already turning towards the door. "I'll see you around, Emma."

He disappeared into the Waterwitch, leaving me to stare at the door as it closed behind him.

Chapter Seven

Jem

I locked the door of the Waterwitch and, for a long moment, just stood there in the dark restaurant, waiting for it to sink in. Emma was here, right here in Cornwall.

She was in a wheelchair.

Emma was in a wheelchair.

God, it was like … like being punched in the gut. Actually, scratch that, I'd *been* punched in the gut, more than once, so I knew how that felt, and seeing Emma just now had been worse. I hoped I hadn't let any of the horror I'd felt show on my face. I hoped I'd at least had the decency not to do that in front of her. Then I realized that, like the world's most selfish moron, I hadn't even asked her how she was. In my eagerness not to mention the wheelchair, I hadn't asked her the most basic, important question of all. She'd even asked me if *I* was OK and I still hadn't managed to remember how ordinary people had conversations with each other.

Being hungry all the time seemed to be turning me into some kind of halfwit. I remembered what she'd said about the footsteps from the first floor and the candle in the window last night and I could feel the throb of a headache starting behind my eyes.

I walked through the restaurant and out to the staircase. Shell was already there, standing on the top step like a pale ghost, her long fair hair reaching down almost to her waist, her eyes seeming too big in her thin face, the cast on her broken arm shining white in the darkness.

"Emma Caine was just here!" she exclaimed, before I could say a word.

"I know. I ran into her outside."

"The cellar door opened! It swung open all by itself!"

"Emma told me," I said. "She thinks the wood must have warped."

"Did you tell her that the door had been nailed shut?"

I shook my head. "Shell, listen, what have I told you about candles after dark? Emma noticed you wandering around last night."

"I heard the woman," Shell said. I could hear the

stubbornness in her voice and my heart sank a little. The throb behind my eyes got worse, too. "I heard her down there again," she said. "Laughing in the cellar."

"Shell," I said, carefully keeping my voice completely level, "there is no one in the cellar."

"Well, how do you explain the door swinging open like that?" Shell asked. "Jem, you nailed it shut yourself!"

I walked over to look at the door and saw that it was open, just a crack. When I grabbed the handle and pulled, it swung forwards easily in my hand. I *had* nailed it shut myself, when Emma's gran had asked me to shortly after I started working at the Waterwitch. I'd used an entire packet of nails on it.

Those nails were no longer embedded in the door, but scattered on the floor at my feet.

I glanced up to where Shell was still leaning over the banisters and said, "All right, look, I won't be cross, but just tell me the truth. Did you pull these nails out yourself?"

"With what? My teeth?" Shell replied, startling me with a rare burst of sarcasm. "I didn't touch them, Jem. They came out on their own."

I bent to pick up a nail and rolled it between my thumb and forefinger. Perhaps the wood warping had caused the nails to fall out...

"There *is* something down there in the cellar," Shell said above me. "I know there is."

I let the nail fall from my hand to roll across the floor at my feet.

Suddenly, I felt the urge to close my eyes and lean my head against the cool, inviting wood of the door. Just for a moment. Just for a moment of total quiet, with no witches, or birds, or laughing cellar people, or nightmares or whatever other demons might be lurking in Shell's head. For the hundredth time, I wondered if I'd done the right thing in bringing her here. But she couldn't go back to Dad. She couldn't ever go back to him again.

I turned away from the door because I was afraid if I kept looking at it then I really might close my eyes and lean against it, and that was something I couldn't do in front of Shell.

I walked around to the foot of the staircase and looked up at her. "Come on," I said. "Come down here and have something to eat."

She joined me and we went through to the kitchen

together, where I made her a sandwich with the last of the bread and cheese.

"Aren't you having anything?" she asked when I put the food in front of her.

I closed the door on the empty fridge.

"I already ate," I lied. My hands were shaking slightly so I shoved them into my pockets. "I'm not hungry."

Chapter Eight

Emma

After leaving the Waterwitch, Bailey and I set off to wander around the cobbled streets and soon came across the ancient, crooked old building that was Looe Museum. The sign outside read: The Looe Museum of Smuggling and Shipwrecks. I'd been inside before, years ago, but I didn't remember it that well and I still had a few hours to kill before I could go and see Gran. Thinking that there might be some stuff in there about the *Waterwitch*, I paid the entrance fee and wheeled myself in. Between what Gran had said about the inn being haunted, and that weird experience with the staircase and the door, I suddenly felt the desire to look into the history of the place a little bit more for myself.

A man sat behind a small desk with words printed in an old-fashioned curling script on the wall behind him:

From Pentire Point to harbour light, a watery grave by day or night.

And, underneath, was a placard saying that around six thousand ships had been wrecked off the Cornish coast. The man behind the desk seemed almost surprised to see me and I guessed they didn't get that many visitors at this time of year.

"You came just in time," he said. "We're closing for the season tomorrow."

The desk was a little high for me to reach so I passed the money over to Bailey who jumped up at the desk to pay our entrance fee.

"He's my assistance dog," I explained. "Is it OK for him to come in with me?"

"Sure, sure." The man waved us through.

The building seemed almost as ancient as the Waterwitch itself. Everything was sloping and crooked and musty, and the wooden floorboards creaked loudly as my wheelchair moved across them. Bailey and I seemed to have the entire place to ourselves. The exhibitions were all pretty old, and didn't look as if they'd been updated in years. I passed through a First World War section that told of how strange lights had been seen off the Cornish coast during the war, and that these were said to be flashed by a Cornishman who'd drowned when his ship had been sunk by a German submarine. Like the wreckers of days-gone-by who'd used lamps to lure unsuspecting ships to their doom on the rocks, the phantom lights of the dead Cornishman were supposed to bring destruction only to German ships and submarines.

I wheeled myself along, hoping to find some information about the *Waterwitch*. Since she was Looe's most famous ship, as well as Looe's most famous haunted inn, I thought they were bound to have something there about it. I wasn't disappointed. Right at the back of the building, there was an entire *Waterwitch*-themed section. I skimmed over the stuff I already knew about Christian Slade and read about what happened to the ship after his death.

While it was still being built, some of the sailors reported that they'd seen the female figurehead move. They'd glance back at her only to find that her head was turned the other way, or that her mouth was suddenly open, as if she was about to say something. Then there was another death when a worker fell from the rigging and broke his neck. People started to say that the ship was cursed.

After it was finished, the *Waterwitch* sat in the

dockyard for a year because no crew wanted to sail her. But it had cost £4,000 to build, which had been a fortune back then, so the brand-new ship wasn't going to be set aside over superstitions forever.

The *Waterwitch* set out on its maiden voyage in 1578 and the stories began soon afterwards. The crew reported seeing a strange woman on board. She'd frequently be spotted at night, on the gun deck or one of the open upper decks. The crew were all men, of course, because it was supposed to be bad luck to have a woman on board. Really, it seemed to me that these sailors had a never-ending list of things that were considered bad luck on a ship. It was amazing they ever managed to get anywhere.

But it wasn't just the common sailors who saw her. Some of the senior mariners saw her, too. There were conflicting stories about what she looked like but most of them never seemed to see her face. Some didn't see her at all but claimed to have heard her laughing.

When the ship docked at Plymouth, some of the crew were so spooked by the phantom woman that they refused to get back on board and new sailors had to be found before the ship could continue.

Not long into the next voyage, one of the nineteen-year-old seamen claimed to have seen the woman but, unusually, he said he had actually seen her face.

Once you see the witch, there's no going back, the placard read. *Once you see her face, it's over.*

He refused to describe what she had looked like and then, a few days later, he tried to jump overboard. When his crewmembers stopped him, he went on a rampage with a musket and shot a whole load of people. Shot them dead, right there on deck, staining the boards with blood and brain splatter. Finally, they managed to wrestle the gun away from him and locked him up. Everyone said he'd gone mad. It was a horrible, blood-soaked history and I thought it was no wonder that people thought the Waterwitch Inn was haunted if it had been built with the timber of such an ill-fated ship.

The poor nineteen-year-old was found dead in his cell a little while later. The accounts were vague about what he'd actually died of but it was thought likely that one of the crew might have killed him, in revenge for the other men who had died during the shooting.

Perhaps that would have been the end of the matter if it hadn't been for the faces in the water.

As the *Waterwitch* sailed towards its next port, the surviving crew reported seeing the faces of their dead shipmates forming in the wake of the ship and the surf that ran alongside it. The faces would appear in the swirling foam for only a moment or two before disappearing, but everyone saw them, or thought they did, even the captain.

At the next port, the entire crew abandoned the ship. The captain refused to set foot on her again and wrote a letter to the admiral of the fleet stating that the *Waterwitch* was a doomed, evil ship and ought to be permanently decommissioned for the sake of common decency.

For another few years it sat in the harbour, not going anywhere and generally creeping out the dockhands, some of whom reported hearing a woman laughing on the boat in the dead of night. I went on to the next placard and read that, eventually, another crew was found for the *Waterwitch*, this time with a no-nonsense captain with decades of experience and a zero-tolerance policy for ghosts, ghouls, phantom women or bloody rampages. He'd hand-picked his crew to make sure they weren't prone to wild superstitions, either. And, because he didn't believe in bad luck, the captain even ordered the ship's name to be changed. It was no longer to be called the *Waterwitch*, but was to be known as something else instead. There was no record of the new name – it seemed to have got lost somewhere in all the history books.

Although the captain ordered the ship's name to be changed without a second thought, the dockhands weren't quite so happy to court bad luck in this way and no one wanted to be the one to go and paint over the *Waterwitch* name. The first man who agreed to do it somehow got caught up in the ropes of the platform and ended up hanging himself. The second man managed to finish the job but came back saying there was something wrong with the figurehead, and that nothing would possess him to ever go back on to that ship.

In 1582, the newly christened ship set out on its last-ever voyage and promptly vanished, not to be seen or heard from again until it was discovered drifting deserted in the mist two years later...

The sound of footsteps made me look round in surprise. I hadn't seen another soul in the museum while I'd been there, but it was only the man from the front desk.

"Just wanted to let you know that we're closing in five minutes," he said. "Did you see everything you wanted to see?"

"Yes," I said. "It was mainly the *Waterwitch* stuff I was interested in. My grandmother owns the inn."

"Wouldn't catch me staying at that place," the man grunted.

"Why not?"

"Too many stories," he said. "I never used to take much notice until a friend of mine stayed there one time. Not the superstitious type at all, even though he was a fisherman. Never believed in bad omens or ghosts or anything like that. He was supposed to be staying at the Waterwitch for a week but, the first night, he checked himself out at 3 a.m. Came knocking on my door wanting a bed for a night."

"Why did he check out?" I asked.

"He said he woke up to find two sailors there in the room, trying to put his boots on for him." He shook his head. "Anyone else had told me that − I mean *anyone* − and I just would've laughed at 'em. But Frank, I mean, he probably dreamed the entire thing, but this was a man who regularly volunteered for the coastguard and thought nothing of going out into the ocean in storms that could easily sink the whole damn ship."

I shrugged and said, "I used to visit the inn when I was a kid and I never saw anything."

"Well, it's closed now, ain't it? Been shut up like that for two months. But I've heard people say they've seen lights turn on in the middle of the night, like there's someone in there."

I thought of that lit candle. But I'd only seen it for a moment and I couldn't be completely sure that it hadn't just been a reflection from a street lamp like Jem had said.

"Phantom lights, they call them, when they're seen at sea," the man went on. "And the Waterwitch is part ship still, ain't it? Unnatural place – sitting there on dry land like that, trying to convince people it's not a ship at all."

He went off to lock up the museum, and I was relieved to get away from him and out into the fresh air.

Chapter Nine
Shell

After lunch I went back to my room and took the poppets from their hiding place in the wardrobe. I'd made the dolls a couple of years ago, during a particularly bad time with Dad. One day I'd been up in my room when I heard him yelling at Jem downstairs, then there was a crash and a thump and I knew it had turned violent again. Sure enough, Jem came upstairs a short while later, and he was moving stiffly, and his breathing sounded funny, and he had one hand pressed over his ribs.

I tried to ask how badly he was hurt but he just waved my concern away and said, "Don't go downstairs for a little bit, OK? Stay up here. Out of the way."

That was when I decided I had to do something to try to help. So I made two poppets – one each for Jem and me. Mum's old witchcraft book said that the more love you put into them, the more effective the spell, so I spent hours making the small dolls, taking special care with Jem's.

I sewed them out of cloth cut from an old pillow-case, filling the bodies with dried herbs, lavender sprigs and a rose quartz crystal for protection. Then I took hair from Jem's brush and nail clippings from his bin and sewed those in, too. To strengthen it even more I made the doll some clothes out of one of Jem's old T-shirts, drew hair on the head and used different-coloured buttons for eyes. Then I read out the spell from the book:

I hereby link this poppet to Jem Penhale. Let any harm directed at him from the physical or magical worlds fall upon the poppet instead so that it may gather up any evil sent to him and return it back from whence it came.

I didn't tell Jem about it because he didn't like anything to do with witchcraft, but it didn't work anyway. The poppets couldn't protect us from Dad, they didn't make any difference at all. Maybe I hadn't done the spell right. Maybe this wasn't the kind of thing you could teach yourself how to do from a book. I'd spent so long making the poppets, though, that I felt attached to them anyway and brought them with us when we came to the Waterwitch.

They still smelled of herbs and lavender, and the

scent reminded me of Mum and made me feel safe. I took them over to the dressing table, sat on the stool and lit my last stick of myrrh incense. It was meant to be good for protection so I dowsed the poppets with the smoke every now and then. Maybe it didn't make any difference but it couldn't hurt, either, and just the ritual of doing it made me feel better. Because you just never knew with Dad. You never knew when he might take it into his head to come after us and hurt us some more.

When Emma's gran had changed her mind and sent us the keys for the Waterwitch, it had almost seemed like a miracle. Having somewhere to go, somewhere to hide, just when we needed it most – it was like there was some kind of guardian angel looking out for us. If it wasn't for the woman down in the cellar it would almost be perfect. I could feel her watching me sometimes. Perhaps it was because she could tell I was a witch like her. Whenever I handled the poppets I could sense her closer than ever, and this time was no different. It actually felt as if she was in the room with me. There was no sign of her at all but that prickling feeling couldn't have been any stronger if she'd been sitting on the stool right beside me…

Suddenly my eyes took in the image of my own reflection in the mirror, and my breath caught in my throat in sudden shock. I could see myself sitting at the dressing table, but the reflection wasn't right. My hands were resting in my lap, but the me in the mirror was gripping the incense stick like it was a knife and stabbing the smouldering tip right into Jem's poppet.

The smell of something burning seemed to hit me like a physical blow and, when I looked down, I saw to my horror that the mirror was right after all. My hands weren't resting in my lap like I'd thought. I really was holding the incense stick and the tip was pressed into the poppet's right hand. I jerked the incense away and plunged it into a nearby glass of water but it was too late. It had already burned through the thin cloth, leaving behind a blackened circle, the herbs and lavender inside shrivelling up into charred ash.

I leaped from the chair so fast that it fell over. Turning away from the smoking poppet on the dressing table, I raced straight from the room and down the stairs to look for Jem. They might have been protective poppets but they were still linked magically to the person they resembled and I was terrified that I might find Jem with his hand burnt or mangled or terribly injured. But when I ran into him by the front door he seemed completely fine. My eyes went straight to his hands and they looked normal.

"Did you pick those nails up off the floor?" he asked. "When I went back to get them they were—"

"Are you OK?" I cut him off. "Is your hand all right?"

He stared at me. "Er ... yes. Last time I checked. Why?"

"Oh. No reason. Nothing. Never mind."

"Did you take the nails from the cellar door?" Jem asked again. "I can't find them anywhere."

"No. I don't have them. Maybe they rolled through the cracks between the floorboards?"

"Maybe." Jem frowned, then shook his head. "I have to go or I'll be late for my shift. I'll see you later, OK?"

I said goodbye to Jem and then went straight upstairs to mend his poppet. The scent of lavender mixed horribly with the acrid smell of burning. Some of the herbs had spilled out of the split hand but I put the non-burnt ones back in, fastened a patch over the charred cloth and silently gave thanks that no harm had been done.

Chapter Ten

Jem

I hung my coat up in the staff cloakroom and then went into the kitchen. It hadn't got really busy yet but there was still plenty of activity going on, and it felt good to be around normal people doing normal things. For the first half hour or so I helped with clearing up what was left of lunch before going out to take orders from the guests in the lounge. Someone asked for a pot of tea so I picked up one of the silver teapots on my way back through the kitchen and went over to the big industrial water boiler in the corner. The red caution light was on, and a notice stuck on the side warned that the water inside was scalding.

I flipped the teapot lid open to throw in the teabags, but when I held the pot up under the spout and lifted the red lever to release the water, it didn't run straight into the pot like I'd expected. It couldn't because, somehow, the lid was closed, blocking the way.

I guess I must have closed it without thinking. The boiling water gushing out had nowhere to go except straight down the metal sides, pouring over my fingers and down my wrist, soaking the sleeve and scalding my skin. Everyone in the kitchen must have heard my yell and the crash as the teapot fell to the ground.

And there was something wrong with the boiler because, even though I'd released the red lever, the flow of water didn't stop like it was supposed to. It suddenly blasted out everywhere in a loud spray of scalding droplets that I only just managed to avoid as I lunged over to turn the machine off at the mains.

One of the chefs saw what happened and hurried over. "What the heck was that?" she said. "That thing only got serviced last week. Get your hand into cold water right away. And someone put an *Out of Order* sign on that boiler. I don't want anyone touching it until we find out what's wrong."

It wasn't a serious burn but, as I held my smarting hand under the cold tap, I remembered how Shell had come running down the stairs earlier and asked if my hand was all right. If I didn't know any better, I'd almost wonder whether she really had seen the future in one of her witch balls.

Chapter Eleven

Shell

My bedroom still smelled of burnt lavender an hour after putting the poppets back in the cupboard. It was a horrible, cloying scent and I was sure I could smell it on my skin and in my hair, so I went to have a shower to wash it off. I tied a plastic bag over my cast and then stepped beneath the hot water. It felt good just to stand there in the steam and let the water run down me. At some point, my foot pressed against the plug and I felt it click into place in the bath. I tried to pull it back out but the plug seemed to be stuck so I left it and turned back to the showerhead. I wasn't going to be in here much longer anyway.

I ran my hand through my wet hair and closed my eyes, enjoying the warmth and the soft sound of the shower filling up the bath. Just a few more minutes, I thought. Just a few more minutes and then I would get out.

Something brushed against my foot and I assumed it was the flannel but I couldn't be bothered to move. The water in the bath was ankle-deep now and the flannel was stuck to my left foot. But then something else brushed my right foot. And then the back of my ankle. What was floating in the water down there?

I frowned and opened my eyes.

I looked down, still expecting to see just a flannel and maybe a plastic lid from a shower-gel bottle or something.

But, no.

The water looked black at first and, for a confused moment, I thought there must be ink in it. But then I realized what I was actually seeing.

The bath was filled with wings.

It was filled with wings, filled with wings, filled with wings.

No birds, no beaks or clawed feet, only the wings, sodden and bedraggled and ruined, with strings of blood swirling out between the feathers as they floated limply there upon the surface.

I stared at them for one horrified moment before I screamed and stepped back, trying to get away. My heel trod directly on a wing and I heard and felt the crunch of tiny bird bones breaking beneath my foot.

I splashed towards the side of the bath, desperate to be out of that bloody water and terrified at the thought of slipping over and falling back into the tub where the wings would brush over my bare skin, stroking and tickling like fingers.

I leaped out on to the bathmat, grabbed the nearest thing to hand, which happened to be my hairbrush, and then hurled it at the mirror hard enough to smash the glass into sparkling shards that flew out into the sink.

"*What do you want from me?*" I screamed, but the birds didn't answer and I wasn't surprised because they never did.

How I wished I could be haunted by something normal.

Like ghosts, or bad memories, or whatever it is that normal people are haunted by. But, no, none of those normal hauntings for me.

Instead, I am haunted by birds.

At first I thought that they were just ordinary, like the seagulls I saw all over Looe, pecking at the cobbles and biting the tourists. The first time I realized my birds were different was one afternoon when Dad was driving me and Jem home from school. I was five years old and had been seeing the birds for several weeks. As soon as we pulled into the lane where our fisherman's cottage huddled at the edge of the coast road, I looked up at my bedroom window and saw them again – all these little black birds staring out at me. There must have been fifty of them there, squashed up against the glass. As we pulled into the drive I asked Jem why the birds were in my bedroom.

"What birds?" he said.

I pointed up at my window. They were still there, their eyes shining black beads in their tiny heads that stared unblinkingly down at us.

"There are no birds in your bedroom, Shell," Dad said from the front seat.

I stared at the back of his head in surprise. Were we playing a game? Was that why he was pretending he couldn't see them? But it wasn't like Dad to play games with us. It wasn't like him at all.

"But they're right there," I said. Then I looked up at my window again and saw that they'd gone. *Poof!* Vanished away like the sea mist that blew in from the grey ocean.

As I got older I realized that no one was ever going to believe me about the birds, not my teachers or my classmates or the people in the street. Not even my brother – and if Jem didn't believe me then no one would. No one except, perhaps, for another witch. Perhaps, the witch who haunted this very inn…

The birds were always too still, too silent. They wanted something from me but I could never work out what. I only knew that I should keep my distance – or else something very bad would happen. Something beyond bad.

So when I heard them, late at night, pecking at the window or scratching around under my bed or flapping their wings in the dark, I would pull my quilt up over my head and pretend I couldn't hear them, pretend they weren't even there. Jem said that was the best way to deal with them and I always listened to Jem because I knew that he loved me.

"I can't see you," I'd say to those black faces squashed up against the window, their beaks scraping over the glass. "Go away, I can't see you. Jem says you're not even really there. You're just inside my head."

But it was harder to say those words now. It was

harder to believe them after that day, just over a week ago, when I'd broken my arm. I'd seen them draw blood then – real, actual blood that glistened in red, shiny drops on the floor. And if the birds were just a phantom of my imagination, then how could they make a person bleed?

After hurling my hairbrush at the mirror, I slumped back down on the damp bathmat and sat there shivering for the longest time, feeling trapped and trying not to cry and trying not to cry and trying not to cry. The birds had never appeared in the bath before. That was new. I wondered what other new things they were planning to do. It was almost as if they knew I was used to them by now and that it was going to take more than pressing their faces up against a window to freak me out. And it had got worse since we moved to the Waterwitch. The birds came more often, and they seemed even more restless and agitated than before.

For the billionth time, my mind rushed round and round in circles looking for a way, any way at all, to get Jem to believe me about the birds. But, as always, I came up with nothing. Jem couldn't see them, and if he couldn't see them then he couldn't believe that I saw them, either, and if he couldn't believe that then he couldn't help me.

When I finally stood up and wrapped a towel around myself, the water in the bath was completely normal – swirling with soap and suds rather than feathers and blood – and the plug came out easily when I tugged it.

I went back to my bedroom to get dressed. It took me a bit longer with a broken arm but, once I'd managed to put on a change of clothes, I walked out into the corridor. It had smooth wooden floorboards, brass lights attached to wood-panelled walls, and doors that were designed to look like cabin doors, with portholes painted on to the wood in cracked, faded paint. Right at the end of the corridor there was a large stained-glass window depicting an old-fashioned ship sailing on the sea. A giant squid lurked in the water just below it, tentacles reaching upwards as if it were just about to burst above the surface in an explosion of foam and terror, and wrap those long tentacles all around the *Waterwitch*.

I knew at once that something was different. The corridor was lighter than it should have been. And that was because one of the bedroom doors, right at the end of the corridor, was standing wide open. I knew for a fact that they had all been closed before.

For a moment I stood, hesitating, not sure what to do. I really hated that I was never sure what to do. If only I was a different kind of person – one of those normal, happy girls, a girl who wasn't haunted by birds – maybe then I would be better at all this.

What I *did* know was that there were twenty-six rooms altogether at the Waterwitch and some of those rooms were safe but some of them were, well, they were wrong somehow. When Jem and I had first come here last week, I had started to go round the rooms one day out of boredom but, after what I'd seen in Room 9 and then the other thing I'd seen in Room 22, I'd decided perhaps I wouldn't explore any more after all.

I needed to go and close that door. Otherwise Jem would think I'd been poking into the rooms again when he'd asked me not to. It was no big deal. It was just an open door that was supposed to be closed and I was going to walk right over there and shut it. Besides, it was one of the rooms I hadn't been into yet, and so it could just be one of the normal ones.

My feet creaked on the floorboards as I moved

closer and closer to the doorway, weak sunlight spilling out to pool upon the floor. When I reached it I saw that it was Room 17. I wanted to slam the door shut without looking inside, but if Jem was here then he would glance into the room to check that everything was OK first, so that was what I did, too.

To my relief, the room looked ordinary enough. The only thing that wasn't quite right was that the pictures weren't straight. Like most of the other rooms, this one had several pictures hanging on the walls – not oil paintings like the big scary one down in the restaurant – but framed prints of the *Waterwitch*, sailing at night, or battling stormy seas or, worst of all, wrecked at the bottom of the ocean.

The paintings hung crooked on the walls, each one tilting obviously to the left. Maybe I should have just left the room, but wonky paintings were exactly the kind of thing that seemed to upset me more than most people. I just couldn't bear to go away and leave them like that. It would play on my mind all day. I would *feel* them hanging crookedly up there, even when I was downstairs.

So I stepped into the room and, being careful to stay away from the window like Jem had said,

I meticulously righted each painting so that its frame was exactly straight, *exactly* straight.

Feeling pleased with myself, I walked out and closed the door softly behind me. There. I had sorted the room out, without any help from Jem, without any help from anyone. I was about to walk away when something made me pause.

I could tell. I could tell, even without being able to see them.

I stepped back to the door of Room 17 and threw it open. The paintings were crooked again, every single one of them, all tilted to the left at that awful, unbearable angle. I dug my nails into the palms of my hands and took a deep breath.

I went back into the room, righted the paintings one by one, came out, closed the door, and then opened it again immediately, without even removing my hand from the door handle.

It had happened again. Five different *Waterwitch*es stared back at me from the walls, all at the wrong angle. Suddenly, it made me angry – really, properly angry, angry like Dad used to get – and I stormed back into the room, determined to get those paintings to hang straight even if it took me the rest of my life.

Perhaps the room fed off my anger but it seemed to get even colder in there and then it felt like something was watching me, something was pitting their will against mine, something didn't want me to touch those pictures. Well, too bad. I was touching them anyway.

I'm not sure how long it went on for, always the same pattern – me straightening the paintings only for them to go crooked again the moment I closed the door. It was probably only a few minutes but it seemed like hours. Then there was a hand on my arm and I yelled and spun round but, of course, it was only Jem, home from work and looking at me that way he did whenever he thought I was acting strange.

"I'm here," he said. "It's OK. Tell me what's wrong."

"The pictures," I said, and, all of a sudden – maddeningly – I felt like crying. "They won't hang straight."

With his hand still on my arm, Jem looked past my shoulder into Room 17.

"They look straight enough to me," he said in a level voice.

"Yes, but look what happens when I close the door," I replied.

I closed it and, stupidly, I felt almost excited that now, finally, I would be able to show him something that he would see and believe. Crooked paintings weren't exactly wings in a bathtub, but they were at least a start.

I threw open the door. And, of course, *of course*, the paintings were all hanging exactly level. Every single one of them was perfectly, devastatingly symmetrical. I stared at the paintings, hating them, and hating the room for showing me up like this in front of Jem. Now he would just think it was more of my craziness. He would think that I was losing my mind, just like Mum had. Oh, God, I really was going to cry.

"I'm not crazy," I said, but my voice came out small and wobbly and completely lacking in conviction. Maybe I *was* crazy, maybe the paintings had been straight all along, maybe there had never been any wings in the bathtub at all.

Jem pulled me towards him and hugged me tight. I could feel the beat of his heart through his shirt, and I could smell the chips on his clothes from the Seagull, and finally I felt warm and almost unafraid for the first time that day.

"Of course you're not crazy," Jem said. "Don't ever think that."

But I see things that aren't there, I wanted to say. *What other word for it is there?*

Jem drew back to look down into my face. "Listen," he said. "Everything with Dad, and what happened to Mum, that's a lot for anyone to take, Shell. But you're out of there now. It's just you and me. No one's ever going to hurt you again and I'm never going to leave you. You know that, right? Things will get better, I promise."

I nodded but only because I knew that was what Jem wanted me to do. Things would never get better. Not so long as the birds were there.

"Now," he said, "what happened to your face?"

"My face?" I repeated, baffled. "What do you mean?"

"You've cut yourself." His voice remained perfectly steady but the pressure of his fingers on my arm increased slightly. "Didn't you know?"

I remembered the smashing mirror and the shards of glass. A couple of them must have flown at me. "Oh. Maybe it happened when I broke the mirror."

"How did that happen?"

I couldn't lie to Jem. He would see right through it. "I ... I threw my hairbrush at it."

"Why did you do that, Shell?" he asked, very quietly.

I could feel my face crumpling up like a child's and I couldn't stop myself from crying. "You won't believe me."

I tried to turn away from him but he wouldn't let me, his hand was firm around my wrist. "It was the birds," he said. "It was the birds again. Wasn't it?"

I nodded, tears streaming silently down my cheeks.

Jem looked down the corridor towards my bedroom. "OK," he said. He raised his free hand to run his fingers through his always-messy hair. "OK," he said again. "I have to get back to the Seagull in half an hour but we'll talk about this later. We'll figure something out. Is there still broken glass in the bathroom?"

I nodded. I'd been too busy battling with the paintings in Room 17 to sweep up the mess I'd made.

Jem cleared up the mirror and wouldn't let me help him. When I peered into the bathroom I saw that there were actually quite a few pieces of glass on the floor. It was a wonder I hadn't sliced my bare feet up on them. I could tell by the look on Jem's face as he brushed up the broken shards that he was probably thinking the exact same thing.

Chapter Twelve

Emma

Bailey and I got to Gran's hospice promptly at 3 p.m. The nurses told me that she was having a bad day, but it still took me by surprise when she greeted me from her bed and then said, "Where's your mother? Just parking the car?"

For a moment I could only stare at her. Finally, I said, "Gran, she didn't come. Remember, I told you last night?"

She looked confused for a moment, then made an impatient gesture and said, "Yes, yes, of course. I know that."

I wheeled my chair up to her bedside but, as soon as we tried to continue the conversation, it was obvious her mind was wandering. She kept referring to things that had happened years ago as if they'd been yesterday and, a couple of times, she even seemed to mistake me for my mum.

"I should have locked that cellar door," Gran

said. "I meant to lock it, I really did. But then, all of a sudden, Jem came running upstairs yelling that you'd been hurt, and I went down there, and there was blood seeping out from under the rubble. I'm so sorry, Emma. So sorry…"

To my dismay, she started to cry, and she'd never looked more like a vulnerable old woman to me than she did in that moment.

"Gran, please," I said. "I didn't come here to upset you. And I don't blame you for what happened. It was my own fault. None of that matters any more, honestly."

I could almost sense the nurses glaring at me from the desk outside, probably wondering what the heck I had said to get her so upset. Finally, after what seemed like an age, Gran stopped crying and managed to pull herself together a bit. She kept patting my hand and saying she was glad I'd forgiven her and that it was a great weight off her mind – even though I'd said before, in the first letter I ever wrote to her, that I didn't blame her. It was like she was getting everything jumbled up in her head.

"Perhaps that witch bottle you found really did

have some kind of evil spirit trapped inside it," Gran went on. "You know, the Waterwitch had always been dog-friendly, always, but after that witch bottle got broken the dogs didn't want to come into the inn any more. The owners would drag them in sometimes and they'd just go berserk. There was one dog that howled all night and the people had to check out and go somewhere else."

My mind instantly went to Bailey and the way he had barked at the cellar door.

"And, a couple of months before I closed the inn, people started saying they could hear something down in the cellar. The door kept opening by itself. We had to nail it shut in the end. There's something awful down there, Emma."

I was startled to hear her mention the cellar door, especially after my recent experience with it.

"But, Gran, if the inn is such an evil place, then why did you agree to let Jem be the caretaker there?"

Gran's hand shot out and wrapped around my wrist so hard that I actually yelped in pain. "I didn't!" she said. "Jem asked me if I needed a caretaker for the Waterwitch but I said no, I said *no*! Please tell me he didn't go back there anyway?"

I quickly shook my head. "No, no. He's working at the Seagull."

"But you just said—"

"Sorry, I was getting muddled up but I remember now. Jem said he asked you if he could be the caretaker but you said no."

I had no idea whether Jem had lied to me or whether Gran was getting confused but the safest thing seemed to be to cover for him for now.

"Gran, please, you're hurting me," I said.

She let go and I rubbed at my red wrist.

"I hated turning him down, Emma, I really did," Gran said. "I know why he needs the money, I know that he wants to leave home and take Shell with him. But there are worse horrors in the world than even their father. And Jem and his sister are the last people who should be in the Waterwitch."

"Why?" I asked, frowning.

"They're descendants of Christian Slade, aren't they?" Gran said. "And whatever haunts the Waterwitch hates that man. That's why we had to get rid of the portrait."

I thought of the missing space on the wall where the painting of Christian Slade used to hang and

100

said, "What do you mean, you got rid of it?"

One of the nurses came over just then to serve the afternoon tea and biscuits. I waited till she'd gone, then said, "Gran, what about the portrait?"

"What portrait?" she said, reaching for her tea and looking at me with that unfocused gaze once again, as if she couldn't quite remember who I was.

"The portrait of Christian Slade. You said you had to get rid of it?"

"It was sticky," Gran said.

"The painting?"

"The blood. I thought it was paint at first but paint isn't sticky like that, and it doesn't smell like that, and it doesn't *feel* like that on your skin. It was blood, Emma. Smeared all over the portrait, running down his face. But the eyes were the worst thing – they'd been torn out. Scratched away." She shuddered. "I thought it had to be one of the guests playing some kind of prank. I ordered another print of the portrait and—" She broke off suddenly, one hand going to her mouth.

"And what?" I asked.

"It was delivered to the inn a few days later and I took it into the kitchen to open it, but the blood

101

soaked through the brown paper even as I unwrapped it. The new painting was exactly the same, Emma – I never even got the chance to hang it up on the wall. Something changed a couple of months before I closed the inn. I don't know why but it's not just haunted any more; it's angry, too."

Chapter Thirteen

Shell

After cleaning up the broken mirror in my bathroom, Jem left for work and I went to the library room to try to read. But there was something in my eye, right in the corner, just beneath the skin. Every time I tried to blink it was there, irritating me. I thought it must be an eyelash that had got trapped and I didn't want to lose it because eyelashes were very powerful things for wishes.

I went into the bathroom and squinted in the mirror, using my finger to pull my eyelid slightly away from my eye. As soon as I found that eyelash, I knew exactly what I was going to wish for. The words played over and over again in my mind as I tried to find it:

I wish Dad would change, I wish Dad would change, I wish Dad would change…

In my head I could see Jem and me back home at the fisherman's cottage with him, the three of us together in time for Christmas. Jem said that was never going to happen, that people didn't change, and that I had to stop hoping for a reunion – but you can't *make* yourself stop hoping, can you? We'd already lost Mum – it didn't seem fair that we should lose Dad, too. So I kept searching for that eyelash until my eye was sore and red and raw. Finally, I saw it; a fine, black lash sticking right out of the corner of my eye.

I pinched it between my thumb and forefinger and gently pulled, expecting it to come free at once. Only it didn't come free. Suddenly it was far bigger and thicker than an eyelash and the object I was dragging out from behind my eye socket wasn't an eyelash at all.

It was a feather.

It hurt as I dragged it out, each individual feathered strand feeling like a hundred thousand eyelashes dragging across the delicate surface of my eye. I wished I could stuff the feather back in but it was too late for that now. The only option was to pull it out altogether.

I couldn't help crying the whole time, partly in pain and partly, well, in dismay. But, at long last, the entire feather was out. I threw it into the sink where it lay, curled and bedraggled and damp with tears.

I knew I had to be smarter than the birds that haunted me but I didn't know how to be that clever. I lifted the feather out of the sink and placed it carefully on the little glass shelf below the mirror. It felt strange in my hands – not soft and smooth like you'd expect a feather to be, but kind of sticky and oily instead, and I hated touching it. The birds were something bad. I knew that because the first day I ever saw them was the day I found Mum hanging by her neck from the apple tree. They were lined up along the branches, strangely silent except for the occasional rustle of wings. They didn't ignore me like most wild birds did – instead they all stared straight at me, like they were expecting something, waiting for something.

When Jem found me there a little later he took me into the house and wouldn't let me return to the garden, but I could still hear the birds, pecking at the windows, pressing their beaks through the gap between the floor and the door, brushing their wings over the glass.

And they'd been with me ever since. I could feel their impatience every time they pecked at me, sharper and sharper, even drawing blood, but it didn't help – I still couldn't understand them, I still didn't know what they wanted.

Chapter Fourteen

Jem

It was busy at the Seagull that evening and the restaurant was full. I couldn't stop thinking about Shell and what she might be doing back at the Waterwitch. What if she really hurt herself next time?

But I couldn't turn down the work. Soon it would be low season, and there would be no extra shifts available, or even any at all. I had no idea what would happen to us then.

But, God, this headache. It was like I had one of Shell's birds trapped inside my skull, flapping its wings and trying to find a way out. My burnt hand throbbed, too. Emma came into the restaurant a little while later with her dog. We waved at each other across the room and seeing her cheered me up a bit. Smelling the food was hard, though. A never-ending torture as I went back and forth to the kitchen. I told myself that if I just kept putting one foot in front of the other then, soon enough, the shift would be over and I could go home and check on Shell and go to sleep. And by tomorrow evening there would be money to buy food and we would both go to bed full.

"Jem?"

I looked up and realized that Sam, one of the other waiters, was speaking to me. I got the impression it wasn't the first time he'd said my name, either.

"What?" I asked.

"I said, are you OK?"

"Yes." I blinked. "Why?"

"Well, you've just poured coffee into that wine glass."

I focused on the glass in front of me and realized he was right. Hurriedly, I fetched one of the silver coffee pots and transferred the coffee into it. It was almost 10 p.m. and the restaurant was starting to clear out a little although Emma was still there, by the window with Bailey. I shouldn't have told her that I would pay for fish and chips. What had I been thinking? Where had I thought the money was going to come from for that?

Stupid.

Stupid, stupid, stupid.

I started loading up a tray at one of the empty tables but my hands were shaking again and I couldn't grip the plates properly. They slipped right out of my fingers, clattering together noisily on the tray. I leaned against the table and willed the trembling to stop but, all of a sudden, I felt like a pencil drawing that was being slowly rubbed out.

Sam appeared at my side and said something but I had no idea what it was.

"What did you say?" I asked, and my voice sounded odd, like I was hearing it from underwater.

Sam spoke again but I couldn't focus on the words. It was just noise.

The table needed clearing still. How long had I been here anyway? Wasn't it terribly late? Shell would be worried. She might do something crazy again, something dangerous. I reached out to pick up one of the empty wine glasses but it slipped from my grip before I could get it on to the tray. I heard the shattering of glass, only it sounded like it was coming from a long, long way off.

Get back to work! the voice inside my head was yelling. *Quick, before they realize something's wrong!*

Then a hand clamped down on my shoulder, fingers pressing into my skin, and I thought it was Dad and I jerked away from his touch out of instinct, my heel crunching on the broken glass on the floor.

"Don't!" I raised my arm to try to protect my face from the force of the blow. Only it wasn't Dad standing in front of me, of course, it was Sam, because I was still at the Seagull, wasn't I? It felt more like a dream, perhaps I was asleep, perhaps my shift had finished hours ago and now I was in bed and having some kind of weird nightmare...

I wasn't sure, I couldn't think properly, I couldn't remember what I was supposed to be doing.

But I must be asleep after all because I was lying down, definitely lying down, in bed.

Except the bed felt a lot harder than usual and someone was saying my name and I knew I had to open my eyes and find out what was happening because it might be Shell and she might be in trouble.

I struggled back up to wakefulness and then the hands came, and it felt like they were crawling all over me. There was one on my arm, another on my shoulder, another on my leg, and I knew that, at any moment, those hands could turn into fists that

110

would punch and pummel and thump, hammer and hit and beat—

I got control of my limbs back, finally, and jerked upright, pushing the hands away before they could punch me in the face, or break my nose, or knock out a tooth.

"Jem, mate, you're OK," someone said, and I realized I was on the floor of the Seagull and that there were several people clustered around me, but the first person I saw was Emma, and she looked pissed off for some reason.

"Looks like I got here just in time," she said, leaning forward a little in her wheelchair with a grim expression on her face. "Jem Penhale," she said, "you are going to tell me everything."

Chapter Fifteen

Emma

Luckily, the owner of the Seagull saw what happened and came straight over to tell Jem that he definitely could not go straight back to clearing tables and that he should go and rest in the kitchen and eat something. No arguments.

"I'll wait for you in the lounge," I said. "Come and find me once you're done."

The lounge was deserted by then and Bailey and I settled down by the log fire that was popping and spitting in the grate. Jem appeared soon afterwards, slouching sheepishly with his hands in his pockets. I was relieved to see that he looked a little better – at least a bit of colour had come into his face and he wasn't pale as death, like he'd been most of the evening.

"This is so embarrassing," he began. "But I really am fine. I think it was probably just—"

I shushed him. "Sit there," I said, pointing at the

armchair next to me. He did as he was told and I was pleased that I hadn't forgotten how to use my bossy voice. I pointed a finger at him. "You lied to me earlier," I said. "When I asked if you were all right."

"I *am* all right!" he protested.

"Stop fibbing. I always could tell when you were fibbing. Come here a second."

"What for?"

"Just do it, Jem."

He sighed and leaned forwards. I threw my arms around him and hugged him tight. After a moment, Jem returned the hug and I rested my head against his shoulder. "I wanted to do this before," I said, "at the Waterwitch. But everything felt weird between us so I didn't." I drew back, looked into his face and said, "I know we haven't seen each other for a long time, but I'm still your friend. Tell me what's going on. When I said something to Gran about you being the caretaker at the Waterwitch she was horrified. She told me that you asked but she said no."

Jem gave me a startled look. "She did say no to begin with, but then she changed her mind. The keys arrived the next day in the post. She must have thought about it and decided to give me the job after all."

"Gran sent you the keys in the post?" I asked. "Did she put a note in there or anything to say why she'd changed her mind?"

"No, it was just the keys. They arrived just over a week ago, in an envelope addressed to me."

"But Gran gave me her keys when I went to see her yesterday," I said. "She told me they were the only ones – that the spare set got lost."

"She isn't very well, Emma. I think she's getting confused about things. I mean, she must have sent me the keys. Who else would have?"

I said nothing for a minute. Gran certainly had seemed confused today. Perhaps she had just forgotten, like she'd forgotten that Mum hadn't come with me to visit her.

"I tried to phone her a couple of times," Jem said, "to say thank you and to sort out how I'm going to be paid and stuff. But every time I called the hospice they told me she doesn't want to take any phone calls. I was going to go down there and visit her but I'm not sure that's such a good idea any more. I don't want to somehow give away that Shell and I are staying at the Waterwitch."

"The Waterwitch? You mean you've left home?"

"We had to. Dad broke Shell's arm," he said. "She told the doctors that she fell down the stairs and they believed her. I couldn't let her go back after that. And now Shell is... Where do I start? Do you remember how she used to have those imaginary birds?"

I nodded slowly.

"Well, it's getting worse. The birds are a constant thing with her. She really believes she can see them. It all started the day Mum killed herself. When I found them in the garden there were all these birds on the branches of the apple tree, and Shell had been sitting out there by herself for God knows how long, and I think it scarred some part of her brain. And, before Mum died, she was always filling up Shell's head with all this nonsense about how her family came from a long line of Cornish witches.

"This is the second week we've been at the Waterwitch, and the first one wasn't so bad because she was going to school. But now it's half-term, and there's been work at the restaurant so I haven't been there as much. She just wanders around the inn all day and I guess all the ghost stories about the place are getting to her. She's seeing things, hearing things."

He put his head in his hands suddenly. "I know she needs help but no one understands her like I do. I can't risk her being taken away. If I go to the authorities then that's what will happen. They'll take her and they won't know how to look after her."

"So what's your plan, then?" I asked.

Jem looked up. His green eye still caught me by surprise. "I'll be eighteen soon," he said. "I can look after her. I just need to save up enough money for a deposit before we move out of the Waterwitch."

"Shell's always been a bit different," I said. "And all that crap with your dad probably made it worse. Now that it's just the two of you, she'll get used to feeling more safe and then maybe she can relax a bit more. She just needs time, that's all."

"I hope you're right," Jem replied.

"So that must have been Shell's candle I saw in the window of the Waterwitch last night? And her footsteps I heard upstairs. It was like an ice box in there. I suppose you don't want to light a fire because people will notice the smoke?"

"No one can know we're there," Jem said. "It was hard enough to convince your gran to let me come in a couple of times a month to check the place over.

She'd never agree to us living there."

"OK, here's what we're going to do. I'm going to move into the Waterwitch with Bailey. It's my grandmother's inn – no one will think it's weird that I'm staying there – and that way I can keep Shell company during half-term and you can light the fires and not freeze to death."

"Would you really do that?" Jem asked.

"Of course," I said. "I'll come over there tomorrow."

"That would ... that would be a massive help," Jem said. "Thanks, Em. Really."

"You don't need to thank me. I'd love to see Shell again anyway."

"I know she'd love to see you. And if she's not there all by herself then perhaps her imagination won't run riot any more. It's a lot easier to imagine things when you're alone in the dark."

Chapter Sixteen

Jem

I said goodnight to Emma and headed home. As soon as I stepped out of the Seagull, I saw that there was a light on in one of the rooms on the top floor of the Waterwitch. That single gold rectangle was painfully bright against the dark façade of the building and I groaned aloud. Shell seemed to find it completely impossible to remember that she mustn't go around turning on lights at night. Still, at least that wouldn't matter any more when Emma came to stay with us tomorrow.

I let myself in through the back entrance, went upstairs to the bathroom and locked the door. Had I actually just fainted at the Seagull? In front of everyone? In front of Emma? I pinched the bridge of my nose. This really was not the way I wanted her to see me at all.

Emma had been my one true friend at school, the only one who had stuck by me through everything

– Dad's drinking, Mum's suicide, all the gossip that came afterwards. The Penhales were a rotten bunch, everybody said so, everybody knew they were trouble and that you stayed away from them. If a supply teacher ever took our class, the moment they discovered my second name they would watch me, waiting for me to disgrace myself somehow – perhaps by stabbing another child in the eye with a pair of scissors, or flushing the pet hamster down the toilet, or setting the building on fire.

It was different with Emma. She didn't seem to care that I was a Penhale. She didn't see me that way at all. After we became friends, it became a bit easier with some of the other kids, and we even became friends with a boy called Ben, who joined our group and made us into a threesome for a while. The whole time I was at school I only had a friend round to my house to play once. It was before Mum died, when I was about seven years old. I wanted to invite Emma but Mum said that Dad would be more likely to agree to it if I asked a boy, so I asked Ben. We played in the garden and Mum made us fish fingers for tea. It was nice. It was normal.

Until Dad got home from work. We all knew the

moment he arrived because he slammed the front door so hard that the walls shook. Ben jumped in his seat and dropped his fork. I remember crossing my fingers and trying to cross my toes inside my slippers, hoping and hoping that Dad wouldn't shout while Ben was here, that he would wait until my friend had gone home.

But Dad didn't care that Ben was there. He'd just picked Shell up from her friend's house and there'd been some upset when the other girl wouldn't believe Shell about being a witch. The friend's mother had had a word with Dad about it and now he was livid, like he always was whenever the subject of witchcraft came up in our house.

"Do you want us to be the laughing stock of the whole town?" he screamed.

Ben was staring at him open-mouthed and I remember thinking, *God, don't stare, don't make eye contact, don't draw attention.*

But Dad wasn't interested in us just then. He grabbed Mum by the hair – it was always her hair; never her arm or her hand. She'd plaited it with some of her favourite flowers – bird's-foot trefoil with their bright, butter-yellow petals – but the flowers fell loose as he dragged her out of the room. I remember staring at them on the floor as Ben and I listened in silence to the sound of Dad slapping her in the living room.

Three times.

Slap.

Slap.

Slap.

The most terrible sound in the whole world.

"I don't care if you really believe all that witchcraft crap, just keep your mouth shut around the kids, you stupid bitch," Dad said – quietly this time – but we still heard him from the kitchen and his quiet voice was just as bad as his shouting one, the soft words echoing over and over again inside my head as I sat there at the kitchen table.

Stupid bitch.

Stupid bitch.

Stupid bitch.

How could he speak to her like that?

I looked up and saw that Ben was watching me with a mixture of horror and fascination, like I was some awful bug that had crawled out from underneath a rock.

Mum came back into the kitchen a moment later. There were no flowers in her hair any more but she tried to disguise the fact that she'd been crying as she said in her fake-cheerful voice that it was time for her to take Ben home.

When we got to his house, the car had barely stopped moving before he was leaping out of it and running up the front drive without a backward glance. I didn't blame him, but I wished I'd never invited him round for tea.

Mum sighed and rested her hand gently on my knee. "I'm sorry, Jem," she said.

I knew she meant it, that she really was sorry, and it made me feel sick that Dad had hit her again and that I hadn't even tried to help. But, still, in that moment, I hated Mum a little bit, too, for doing and saying the things she must surely have known were guaranteed to make Dad go berserk. She shouldn't have told Shell she was a witch, she should never have mentioned witchcraft at all. I couldn't forget that look I'd seen on Ben's face – that disgust mixed with fear. As the car pulled away I stared out of the window at Ben's cosy-looking home and wished I was in there with him, wished I never had to go back to my own house again.

The next day, the whole school knew about what had happened. Kids kept running up to me, laughing and teasing me about Mum being a witch and Dad being a criminal.

"He's *not* a criminal!" I said, even though I had no idea why I was defending him.

Ben avoided me all morning, moving right over to the other side of the classroom. Every time I looked at him, he was whispering to other kids, and looking over at me. And sniggering.

It was the sniggering that hurt the most. It wasn't funny to me – in fact there was nothing in the entire world that was less funny than Dad in one of his rages – but maybe it was something you could laugh at when you didn't have to live with it.

"What's wrong with Ben?" Emma had asked. She was sitting next to me, helping me paint a giant picture of a car.

"I don't think we're friends any more," I replied, before grabbing a paintbrush and bending over the painting so that I wouldn't have to look her in the eye.

I knew that Ben would tell Emma about what had

happened and then I'd lose her, too. Sure enough, at break time, he came over to where the two of us were sitting on the grass and said he wanted to talk to Emma. *Alone.*

Emma gave me a puzzled look but she got up and walked over to the other side of the playground with him. I watched him talking to her, helpless to stop it. Emma would find out what had happened and then she probably wouldn't want to be friends with me, either.

But then, to my astonishment, Emma suddenly lifted both hands and shoved Ben so hard in the middle of his chest that he fell straight down, skinning his elbow on the ground.

"You're a rubbish friend," she shouted. "I never liked you anyway! You're mean!"

Seeing the blood on his elbow, Ben instantly burst into tears and a teacher soon came running over to help him up and scold Emma. I couldn't hear what they were saying but I saw Emma cross her arms over her chest, stony-faced, and shake her head and I guessed that she was refusing to apologize.

Finally, the teacher took Ben, still crying, inside, and Emma came over to throw herself back down on the grass beside me.

"We're not friends with Ben any more," she announced.

"Was he telling you about last night at my house?" I said.

She nodded.

"It's true," I whispered. "Dad went crazy again."

"So what? I'm never speaking to him again. I like it better when it's just us." She threw her arms around me and said, "You're my most favourite friend, anyway. My *best* friend."

I gripped the sink and stared into the bathroom mirror and my green eye seemed like it belonged to someone else – even after all these years I hadn't really got used to it, still didn't expect to see it there in the glass – and I couldn't believe, I just couldn't believe that I had made such an idiot of myself in front of Emma tonight.

But staring despairingly into the mirror wasn't going to help with that so I finally picked up my toothbrush to clean my teeth. I was just reaching to turn the tap off afterwards when I froze.

For a moment – for just this one crazy moment – it looked like there were faces in the water swirling around the bottom of the sink. Faces that gurgled and spluttered down the plughole, carried away into the drains.

God, what was the matter with me? For a while back there at the Seagull, I really hadn't known where I was or what I was supposed to be doing. Now I was seeing faces in the sink. Perhaps Shell wasn't the only one who was cracking up. Perhaps it was happening to both of us, only I just couldn't recognize it in myself.

It was definitely a good thing that Emma was coming tomorrow. With her around, things could only get easier.

Chapter Seventeen

Shell

I went to bed after Jem arrived home from the Seagull but, just a few hours later, I was woken by a noise from downstairs. I got up and went straight next door to Jem's room to tell him there was someone in the inn with us, but his bed was empty and didn't look like it had been slept in at all. It must have been him who'd made that noise. Wondering what he was doing up in the middle of the night, I went down to the restaurant and instantly saw light spilling out from the open kitchen doorway.

I walked past the empty tables and into the kitchen. For a confused moment I thought it was full of sea mist, but then I realized it was actually steam. The bright neon strip lights above were switched on and I saw Jem, standing at the far side of the kitchen with his back to me. He was fiddling with one of the kitchen appliances – one of the big gleaming metal ones that hadn't been turned on since the

Waterwitch closed down.

"You scared me," I said, wondering how long he had been here. "What are you doing?"

Jem didn't reply and, in the silence, I heard a hissing sound from whatever that kitchen thing was. I suddenly had a really, really bad feeling.

"Jem?"

"Everything's fine, Shell," he said, but his voice sounded wooden and stiff and not like him at all.

I heard water splashing and realized the machine he'd turned on was the industrial water boiler, and that's where all the steam was coming from.

"What have you switched that on for?" I asked, taking a step closer.

For the first time, I saw that water was running straight on to the floor at Jem's feet. Frowning, I walked over to see what he was doing.

It was so awful that, for a long moment, I couldn't take it in at all.

Jem wasn't making tea like I'd assumed. Instead he was washing his hands in the gushing stream of boiling water. It bubbled over his skin, which was red and inflamed and bleeding, scarred with raw flesh and white, shiny blisters. He was scrubbing at his hands as if he thought they were covered in soap, and, as I watched, a huge chunk of flesh came right off, landing on the floor with a wet slap, exposing the white bone beneath the ruined red skin.

I grabbed his arm and yanked him away, but, when I went to speak, the voice that came out wasn't mine: "*Evil blood!*" I heard myself hiss. "*The world needs no more men like you!*"

"Everything's fine, Shell," Jem whispered. "Everything's fine."

I woke up then, jerking upright in my bed. It was a long, long time before I managed to get back to sleep.

Chapter Eighteen

Emma

As soon as I wheeled myself through the front door of the Waterwitch, Shell practically threw herself at me, her unbroken arm squeezing tight around my shoulders.

"I'm *so* happy to see you!" she said. "Oh, wow, is that your dog? What's his name?"

"Bailey," I replied. "And it's good to see you, too."

"I'll be back at four," Jem said. "You know where I am if you need me."

He closed the door and then it was just Shell, Bailey and me.

"Is he friendly?" Shell asked, peering at him.

"Oh, yes. Tickle his tummy and he'll love you forever."

Shell smiled and reached out tentatively to stroke her fingers down Bailey's neck. He responded by trying to flick his tongue out at her.

"Do you want to come and see my witch balls?" Shell asked.

"Witch balls?"

"I collect them. Most of them are in my bedroom upstairs but I couldn't fit them all in so I put the spare ones in Room 6 on the ground floor. They move around at night sometimes, so don't worry if you hear them rolling up and down the corridors. I think it's just all the magic stored up inside them."

I had no idea what she was talking about but I wheeled myself through the restaurant behind her. Halfway across I realized Bailey wasn't following us but was unzipping my bag where it lay on the floor by the door.

"Hang on a sec," I said to Shell. "Bailey wants his bear."

Shell stopped. "His what?"

"It's his favourite cuddly toy."

A moment later, Bailey found his grizzly brown teddy and trotted over to us with the toy held carefully in his mouth.

"He probably feels safer with it," I said, feeling obliged to explain. "Even though you're too old for teddies now, aren't you?"

Bailey wagged his tail at me and the three of us went out into the corridor. The cellar door, I noticed, was closed this time.

Shell opened the door to Room 6 and snapped on the light.

A hundred different colours winked back at me like a hundred glass eyes.

The witch balls were piled up in bowls on the windowsill and the dressing table and even by the side of the bed. A giant basket of them stood on the floor in the corner and some tiny ones rested on one of the pillows. I saw purple, green, orange, blue, red, gold and black glass spheres. A few were as big as bowling balls, while some were no larger than an egg.

"Here," Shell said, picking one up and thrusting it into my hands. "See what you can do with this."

The witch ball was cold against my skin and heavy in my hands. At first glance it was blue but when I looked closer I could see that the glass was shot through deep within with swirls of silver and green.

"What am I supposed to do with it?" I asked.

"Witch balls help you see things," Shell replied, picking up a purple one from a nearby pile. "Things that happened in the past or will happen in the future. Or things that happen just out of sight, in the moments when your back is turned or when you have to blink."

She ran her fingers over the cool glass surface of the purple ball in her hands. "If I stare for a really long time, sometimes I can see things in the glass."

"Like what?"

"Like the *Waterwitch*. Back when it was a ship. Drifting in the middle of the sea."

"I can't see anything," I said, handing the blue witch ball back to her. "It's very pretty, though."

She was obviously encouraged by my interest because she said, "I'll show you my poppets, too. Wait here a sec."

She hurried from the room and I heard her take the stairs outside two at a time, coming back a few minutes later with a pair of dolls she had obviously made herself. I could see she must have spent hours making them, even giving them hair and clothes – but there was something about them that seemed a little creepy to me. Perhaps it was the limp, lifeless way they flopped around.

"Are these meant to be you and Jem?" I asked as she thrust them into my hands.

"Yes!" Shell beamed at me. "They're poppets. I put a protection charm on them to help keep us safe."

"They're lovely," I said dutifully. The Shell doll rested on my lap but I picked the Jem one up to examine it closer – and felt the weirdest sensation against my skin – a sort of wriggling feeling, as if there were maggots squirming around beneath the cloth, trying to get out. "Shell, what's inside these dolls?" I asked, alarmed.

"Mostly lavender and dried herbs," Shell replied. "That's why they smell so nice."

I looked back at the poppet in my hand and the button eyes stared back at me blankly. I couldn't feel anything from the cloth body now, though, and told myself I must have imagined it. Even Shell wasn't crazy enough to sew maggots up inside a doll.

"You'll sleep in one of the downstairs rooms, won't you?" Shell asked, taking back the poppets and slipping them into her pocket.

"I kind of have to," I replied, tapping the arm of my wheelchair.

"Don't take Room 7," she said.

"Why not?" I asked.

"There's something not very nice in there," she replied. "You might not be able to see it — I'm not sure — but, I mean, the point is that it will still see you. And it's not the only thing here. I don't know if you were planning to look into the rooms at all but, um ... don't go into Room 7 or Room 9. They're the haunted ones."

"Oh. But what makes you think—"

"I'll help you pick out a room," she cut me off. "One that's safe."

I followed her back out to the restaurant to collect my bag and, this time, I glanced at the big oil painting of the *Waterwitch* hanging over the fireplace.

Then I did a double take.

It sounded crazy, but I had the strangest, most insistent feeling that something in the painting had changed since the last time I'd seen it. Then it came to me all at once — the ship had been facing the other way before. Surely the prow, with its wild-eyed woman figurehead, had been facing the left side of the painting, pointing upwards towards the top corner?

But now it was definitely, unmistakeably, facing the right-hand side.

"It's a horrible painting, isn't it?" Shell said, following my gaze.

"It's a bit … overpowering," I agreed. I must have remembered it wrong. Paintings didn't move.

"It's a lie, too," Shell added.

"Hmm? What is?"

"The hands."

"What hands?"

"In the water." She pointed and, for the first time, I realized that there were pale hands reaching up out of the dark stormy sea.

I peered closer. "Is that … is that supposed to be the missing crew?"

"I guess so. The painting wants us to think that they drowned in a storm. But I don't think that's what happened at all. They'd have taken the lifeboats, wouldn't they? If the storm was that bad? And the lifeboats were all still there on the *Waterwitch* when they found her."

Drifting, deserted in the mist…

"What do you think happened to the missing sailors then?" I asked and then, hazarding a guess, I added, "Mermaids?"

"I saw a mermaid once," Shell said. "In the cove

at Polperro. It wasn't very nice. Its mouth was full of teeth. Just ... full of them. Sharp and vicious-looking, like it would rip your throat right out if it got half the chance. I hope I never see a mermaid ever again as long as I live."

"Um, well, that's..." I racked my brain, desperately trying to think of something to say.

But Shell just smiled and said, "It's OK. No one else believed me, either. Jem said it must have been a seal I saw. But, you know, seals don't have that many teeth, do they? Mermaids weren't involved with the *Waterwitch*, though."

"Well, what do you think happened to the missing crew then?" I asked again. "If you don't think that they drowned, or were killed by mermaids, then what's left?"

There was mutiny, of course, or some kind of insurance-plot conspiracy but I was fairly sure Shell would go for one of the crazier answers like a kraken. Or maybe aliens.

Instead she said, "I think the sailors are all still here. I think that they never left the ship."

Chapter Nineteen

Emma

Shell decided that I should take Room 3, and helped me move my bag there.

I noticed the smell as soon as I went in. It wasn't unpleasant as such, it was just ... odd. A smell of salt, seaweed, brine and the faintest whiff of rot. I had to force myself not to wrinkle my nose. Perhaps it was something to do with the inn having been shut up for two months with no heating on – leaving dampness to creep in everywhere. As a child I'd never stayed overnight at the inn because our house was only a ten-minute drive away.

"This room is OK," Shell told me. "Except for the moon."

"The moon?"

"If you look out of the window from this room, you'll always see a full moon, even if it's really a new moon or a half moon or whatever. I think it's because it must have been a full moon the night the

Waterwitch sank." She shivered and said, "Isn't it cold still? I think I'll go and light the fire in the library."

"Shell?" I said as she was about to leave.

"Yes?"

"What's wrong with Room 7?"

She paused in the doorway. "Don't go in there, Emma."

"I just want to know what—"

"Christian Slade is in Room 7. It's where he hides from the witch. A priest stayed in that room a couple of months before the inn closed and he blessed it before he left."

"How do you know that?" I asked. I remembered what Gran had said about something changing at the Waterwitch just a couple of months before it closed.

"I read it in one of the online reviews. The witch can't get in ... that's why Christian hides in there. It makes her fearfully angry but there's nothing she can do. She hammers at the door, though. All night sometimes. She loves him, you see. But she hates him, too." She glanced at me and said, "Have you ever loved someone and hated them at the same time?"

"No." I shook my head. "I don't think so."

"I'm glad," Shell said fiercely. "It's the worst feeling in the world."

Before I could reply, she went off to look for the matches. I waited for her to be out of sight and then wheeled myself out into the corridor. Room 7 was just a few doors down from my room and I couldn't resist opening the door to have a look. Of course, there was absolutely nothing out of the ordinary there. It looked practically identical to all the other rooms, with a neatly made bed, and a wardrobe and a dressing table.

I pulled the door closed and that's when I noticed the scratches. I peered closer and saw that they looked like claw marks – deep grooves worn into the wood, almost as if there really had been someone out here, desperate to get inside, tearing at the wood with their fingernails. I shook my head. It must have been a dog.

Bailey and I made our way to the library. I couldn't reach the light switch so Bailey jumped up against the wall and turned it on for me. I looked around, remembering how endlessly fascinating it had seemed to me as a child. There was a little bar over in the corner, and shelves lining the walls, filled with raggedy old books. There were worn leather armchairs and patched-up chesterfields tucked into corners or set before the cast-iron wood-burning stove in the corner. I remembered how guests would drink coffee here in the morning, or sip nightcaps after dinner, back when the inn was still open. Curios and knick-knacks filled the space between books on the shelves. They were all sea-themed in some way or other. I saw messages in bottles, ivory pieces of scrimshaw and glass mermaids. But the light fixture was the strangest thing of all.

It was a massive wooden model of the *Waterwitch* ship, suspended from the ceiling with all its portholes lit up with a sickly yellow light. It wasn't really enough to illuminate the small room and so there always used to be candles lit on the tables, too.

You could tell the light fixture was meant to be the ghost-ship version because the sails were in tatters, and masses of barnacles clustered around the prow and the hull like some kind of fungus. The only person on board seemed to be the witch. I could see her little wooden figure peering over the side of the ship – a proper old hag with warts and a crooked snarl and a pointy hat.

I wheeled myself over to the bookshelves. Normally, I loved old books – the soft feel of their frayed covers, the textured paper, the musty smell. But these had obviously all been selected to tie in with the *Waterwitch* myth, and as I looked at the shelves I saw nothing but volume after volume about shipwrecks, sea creatures, ghost ships and water witches.

I picked up the nearest book and opened it to a random page. I was met with a ghastly black and white drawing of a witch being burned to death in a boiling cauldron while a crowd of villagers looked on, cheering and applauding. Some were even waving hankies over their heads in celebration. The witch's face was terrible. She was an ugly old crone with a long beak of a nose but it was her expression that really chilled me. Her eyes were screwed up tight and her mouth was open as wide as it would go – enough to unhinge the jaw – in an agonized silent scream. I could almost hear it, echoing inside my head.

"I've got the matches!" Shell called out, coming into the room behind me.

I snapped the book shut and put it back on the shelf. "Great. Let's get this place warmed up."

Chapter Twenty

Shell

We soon got the fire roaring and it instantly made the room seem a hundred times more cheerful. Bailey lay down in front of the stove with his teddy and that made it even better. Emma and I sat there talking about nothing very much for a while, and it was nice. I'd always liked Emma. She'd never been mean to me or treated me like a freak – not like the other kids at school.

Then Emma asked me what was wrong with Room 9, and I was trying to work out how to reply, or whether I even *should*, when my eyes were drawn by a movement in the wood-burning stove. At first I thought it must just have been a red flash of hot ash, a spark lit up against the black logs.

But then my perception shifted and I saw that those black shapes in the wood-burning stove weren't logs at all. They were birds.

They were writhing in agony in the flames, their

wings catching alight and shrivelling the feathers away into ash while their beaks rapped ferociously against the glass window, desperate to get out, even while their beady black eyes burst in their heads from the heat.

I closed my eyes firmly shut for a moment and, when I opened them, the birds were gone.

"Shell?" Emma said. "Are you OK?"

"Yes!" I stood up. "I have to … go and brush my hair. I'll see you later."

"Oh. OK."

I walked out quickly, without looking at the fire in case the birds reappeared. I ran up the stairs to my room, closed the door behind me and pressed the heels of my hands against my eyes.

"Go away, birds," I muttered, just like Jem had told me to. "You're not real. Go away, go away. I can't see you. You're not there."

I remembered how the birds came again the day Jem's eye changed colour. I was eight and Jem was eleven and Dad had taken us to the beach. As we were leaving to go back home, I asked if I could have an ice cream. Dad snapped at me for holding them up, but he gave Jem the money and said we could have one each.

We both chose a Mr Whippy with a flake in it, then got into the back seat of the car and started the drive home. It was hot and that made the ice cream melt faster. I wasn't eating it fast enough, and some of it ended up getting spilled on the back seat. The moment it happened, Jem's eyes met mine and I guess we both knew what was going to happen next. Dad saw the mess in his rear-view mirror and made a short, angry, all-too-familiar sound that made me flinch.

"Sorry, Dad," Jem said quickly. "I didn't mean to. It was an accident."

Dad didn't reply, just pulled the car over to the side of the road, and I felt my heart speed up as he stamped around to the passenger side. I knew I should do something, that I *must* say something, that I could not allow Jem to take the blame for me like this because I knew what would happen if he did, I *knew*, but I was so scared that I couldn't do it. Couldn't manage to open my mouth and say the words even though I wanted to say them more than anything. Too afraid. Too much of a coward.

I missed my chance to do the right thing, and then Dad was opening the door and he was grabbing

Jem and shouting. I remember crying Jem's name and trying to hold on to his arm but he pushed me back and muttered something at me, a single phrase under his breath: "Stay in the car."

So Dad dragged him out and then he punched him. I mean he really punched him, for the first time, not a smack or a tap or a slap but a punch with his entire fist – *bam!* – right above his left eye. The whole car shook as Jem crashed into it and then collapsed on the floor in the dust.

Then the birds started. I could hear them up there on the roof of the car, pecking and hammering madly at it until the whole car shook and I feared their beaks would rip straight through the roof.

Dad told Jem to get up, and I hated the way that he said it. Like he wasn't sorry. Like Jem was nothing.

"Get up," Dad said again. "And get in the goddamned car."

Jem tried but that punch must have swirled his brain around because even as he tried to stand he staggered and fell back down on his knees again. Dad grabbed him by the neck of his T-shirt and pulled him up, shoving him into his seat and slamming the door closed.

Jem was crying but they were silent tears – he was always telling me that I would have to learn how to do silent crying, too, with no more hiccups or gasping or whimpering, because we both knew that the sound made Dad angry. The problem was that everything make Dad angry. Sometimes it was the neighbours, or the weather, or the plastic lid on the microwave dinner, or the dog that barked down the road, or the pot holes in the drive, or the weather, or the sky, or the sea. Just the whole world, really. Just the whole entire world. And all that anger was like a fourth person there in the house with us sometimes – a dangerous person who spent most of their time asleep and who we would do almost anything to avoid waking up.

I was crying, too, trying to be quiet and not doing a very good job of it. Jem didn't like for me to see him cry, so he had his head turned away, staring straight out of the window, but he reached across the middle seat and wrapped his hand around mine, and the feel of his warm fingers pressing my palm made me feel just a tiny little bit better, and just a tiny bit less scared.

As we drove away, I threw the rest of my Mr Whippy out of the window. I didn't want it any more. In fact,

I've never much liked ice cream since that day.

The sound of a beak pecking at the window yanked my thoughts out of the past but when I whirled around it was only a plump seagull perched outside on the windowsill. The next second it flew away, and I sat down on the side of my bed with a sigh. My eyes fell on my hairbrush resting on the bedside table. I thought I'd left it in the bathroom...

With a growing sense of unease, I reached out and picked up the brush.

It was clogged full of hair.

Only the hair wasn't mine.

The hair tangled up in this brush wasn't blonde, but coarse and black and thick. Not only were the strands the wrong colour but they were stiff with salt and crusty with, God, were those actually *scabs*? There was blood in the hair, too, I could feel it all of a sudden, damp and sticky on my fingers. I suddenly had an image of a woman sitting at my dressing table, staring into my mirror and dragging my brush over her scalp over and over again, over and over and over, until the hair was all pulled out of her head and the bristles only dragged through bleeding flesh. And she would be laughing all the while, that sound that played and replayed in my nightmares.

I heard it then, for real, the laughter climbing up through the floorboards on thin spider legs – a demented daddy longlegs of a laugh that skittered straight towards me on many-jointed, spindly limbs.

And then, as if on cue, real bugs started crawling out of the hair in my brush. I shrieked and dropped it on the floor, staring appalled as lice and mites came skittering out, disappearing into the cracks in the floor, closely followed by different types of aquatic insects: soft-bodied lacewings and bloated fishflies and waxy water beetles, and others that I didn't even recognize. A horror of compound eyes and sucking mandibles and feathery antennae, all crawling up out of my brush.

I watched them squirm and scrabble away down through the cracks in the floorboards and I bit my tongue, bit it hard, because I was afraid that, if I didn't, I might actually start to howl and then I would never be able to stop.

Chapter Twenty-One

Emma

It was lunchtime and Shell had been gone for about an hour. I decided to call her down to see if she wanted to eat together. Bailey and I left our cosy spot in front of the fire and went back through the restaurant.

As I passed by the big painting of the *Waterwitch* I felt the strongest desire to look at it to see if anything had changed but I refused to give in to the temptation. I did not believe in massive oil paintings that moved around when no one was looking at them. But as I wheeled past I suddenly caught the distinctive scent of ocean. Not just salt water, but seaweed and shells and shipwrecks and the slimy, spiny things that live out of sight below the waves, feeding on the skeletons of mysteriously vanished sailors. It was a salty tang that I could almost taste on my tongue, as if I'd just eaten a plateful of fish.

It was like Bailey could sense it, too, because he

growled as he went past, although it came out kind of muffled because he had refused to leave his bear behind and still had it clamped in his mouth.

"There's probably a window open somewhere," I said out loud.

The inn wasn't that far from the sea, after all. And yet … I couldn't remember ever smelling the sea here before, as a kid. Wherever that ocean smell was coming from, it could not be the painting, and if the dark waves looked as if they were moving, that could only be because I was seeing them from the corner of my eye.

I carried on past it and Bailey nosed open the door that led to the monster staircase.

I heard the crying as soon as I went into the corridor. Quickly, I wheeled myself to the foot of the stairs.

"Shell?" I called. "Is that you?"

It had to be Shell. There were only the two of us here.

"Shell?" I called again. "What's wrong?"

The crying stopped abruptly but she didn't call back down to me.

It would be so great if I could just walk up the

stairs like a normal person and go and find Shell to make sure she was all right. I closed my eyes for a moment, drew in a breath to call again, opened my eyes—

—and froze, staring.

The monster staircase was different.

The carvings had moved.

It was impossible — I mean, I *knew* that it was completely impossible for the carvings to have changed position in any way at all — and yet, when I had sat in this exact spot the day before, there had surely been a giant squid staring back at me with its single, startled, massive eye. Now there was a mermaid, baring its teeth at me. And this was no beautiful half-woman, but a monstrous predator with row upon row of needle fangs, mouth open wide, practically hissing and spitting her hatred right out of the wood at me.

"Emma?" a subdued voice said from above. "Did you call me?"

I looked up and saw Shell standing in the shadows at the top of the staircase.

"Were you ... were you crying just now?" I asked.

I couldn't take my eyes off the mermaid. *Had I remembered the staircase wrong?* There were so many different creatures carved into the wood that perhaps I had just muddled up their positions. That was the likeliest explanation. The alternative was ... well, it was just plain mental, that was all.

Shell sniffed loudly above me. "There were bugs," she said, "in my hairbrush. *She's* been using it."

"She?" I repeated, dragging my eyes away from the mermaid.

"The woman," Shell replied.

"What woman?" I asked, confused. Surely there wasn't a fourth occupant of the Waterwitch that no one had thought to mention to me?

"The woman who haunts the Waterwitch," Shell said. "Didn't you hear her laughing just now?"

I squinted up at her. Light from some unseen window up there sliced diagonally across her body, clearly illuminating her skirt and tights and ballet flats, but her upper body and face remained a shrouded silhouette. "Shell, come down here!" I said. "I can't see you properly up there."

"You must have heard the laugh," Shell pressed. "You must have."

"I didn't hear any laughing," I replied. "Only you crying."

"But you *must* have heard her!" Shell cried, and it really was a cry, all filled up with cracks and wobbly bits and broken, brittle edges.

"Shell, I can't come up there," I said, trying to sound patient. "Please come down."

But then, completely unexpectedly, she threw her head right back and let out a laugh.

If you could even call that sound a laugh. It was unlike any I had ever heard before. High-pitched and shrill and all wrapped up in some cold, cruel madness that made my skin shrivel up into tiny goose pimples. There was something inhuman about that noise, a shrieking quality that was almost bird-like.

It stopped quite abruptly and Shell sounded shocked as she said, "There! Did you hear it?"

I stared at her. "Are you trying to be funny?"

I still couldn't see her face properly but she sounded genuinely confused when she replied, "Didn't you hear it?"

"Come off it. You're the one who laughed."

"Me?" Shell repeated, and she sounded absolutely

aghast. "But that was a *mad* woman's laugh!"

Then, out of nowhere, she threw her head back once more – a strange jerky movement, almost as if someone had just yanked at her hair – and then she laughed again. That same sound that didn't just send shivers down my spine but right into my brain as well. The wooden mermaid on the banister was still baring her teeth at me and, all of a sudden, it looked like there were even more teeth inside her mouth than there had been before.

"There it is again!" Shell exclaimed.

"Shell, I mean it, stop doing that!" I said. "You're freaking me out!"

She laughed and now it sounded more bird-like than ever – a sound that should come from a beak or a gaping maw rather than a mouth. It was an insane noise that made me feel I would do anything to avoid hearing it again, and not just normal things like clamping my hands over my ears or wheeling at speed in the opposite direction, but mad, bad things, like shooting everyone in sight or hanging myself from the first available beam.

"SHELL!" I shouted her name at the top of my voice.

She broke off laughing abruptly. "What?" she said, her voice very small all of a sudden.

"Come down these stairs," I said. "Right. Now."

To my relief, this time she obeyed.

"What are you playing at?" I asked her. I felt freezing cold and had to resist the urge to rub my arms. "I don't ever want to hear that laugh again. Jesus."

Shell stared at me and her eyes looked even larger than normal in her pale face. "But you can't really think that *I* was the one making that awful sound?"

"Shell, I s*aw* you!"

Geez, I was totally out of my depth here. Shell had always been a little strange but this was seriously nuts, proper loony-bin stuff. Maybe she really had cracked up. Maybe Jem should let them take her away.

And yet ... I was the one who thought that painted ships and wooden monsters were moving around.

I rubbed at my eyes and said, "Let's just forget it. I came to see if you wanted lunch. Let's have some food. And then you can tell me about this woman who's been using your hairbrush."

Chapter Twenty-Two

Emma

It was raining outside. Through the windows we could see that Looe was dark and drenched with sea mist, so I assumed that Shell and I would eat at the Waterwitch but, as it turned out, there wasn't any food.

"Jem hasn't gone shopping yet," Shell said.

"All right. Let's go out." I hesitated, then said, "It is OK for you to leave, isn't it? I mean, it won't be a problem if your dad happened to see you?"

Looe was a tiny village and it was a definite possibility that we could run into him by accident.

Shell shook her head. "He works on the fishing boats at night so he sleeps during the day. And, even if we did see him, he wouldn't come over to us. Jem says he's glad we left. Fewer mouths to feed."

"I'm sorry," I said. The words were feeble, but there didn't seem to be anything else to say.

Shell shrugged. "I only need Jem," she replied.

We went out into the drizzle. Bailey must have been happy to be out of the Waterwitch because he didn't seem to mind the rain like he usually did. I had an umbrella thing that attached to my wheelchair, which I hated using because I was sure it made me look truly ridiculous but it was better than getting soaked so I put it up anyway. Dignity was another one of those things you couldn't be too precious about when you were stuck in a wheelchair.

"Don't you have an umbrella or something?" I asked Shell. She had a light rain mac on but she hadn't drawn the hood up and her long hair was already soaked.

She shook her head and said, "I like the rain. Especially when it tastes like the sea. Can we stop here for a moment?" She gestured towards a little shop – one of the many touristy ones in the crooked, cobbled street. "I just want to get some more incense. Don't tell Jem though, will you? I, um, I kind of told him that I don't have any money. And it's almost true – I've hardly got anything left – but if he knew then he'd want to spend it on food and sometimes there are more important things. Jem doesn't understand that. I'm not very good at explaining it to him, I guess."

Without waiting for me to reply, she skipped off across the cobbles, her wet hair dripping down her shoulders, leaving Bailey and me no choice but to follow.

The sign outside the shop read: *Looe's Witch and Mermaid Shop.* I grimaced when I saw how tiny the store was. Every available space seemed to be crammed full of stuff. There was barely room for a wheelchair in there, let alone a German Shepherd.

"Sorry, old boy," I said. "We won't be long."

I told Bailey to stay and then followed Shell into the store. My palms stung as I wheeled myself over the threshold. I sighed. I'd been wheeling myself around a bit more than usual so I was getting blisters on my palms again. A bell hanging above the door tinkled sharply as we entered, and the overpowering smell of incense hit me in the face.

The shelves were crammed with little witches, shell mermaids, black candles, charm dolls, dowsing rods, tiny cast-iron cauldrons, pentacles, sticks of incense – and bottles. A whole wall of them, glinting back at me in different colours, shapes and sizes. The sign next to them said that they were a selection of witch bottles, spell bottles and wish bottles.

There was a girl sitting behind the till, perhaps a year older than me. She was extremely pretty, with dark hair that was almost as long as Shell's, and large blue eyes lined with dark make-up. Her hair was loose but some of it was tied back into plaits, set with mottled blue and white sodalite beads carved to look like mermaids. She wore a black dress with chunky lace-up hiking boots. It was a cool kind of look I never would have been able to pull off myself, even before the wheelchair. The dress was sleeveless, so I could clearly see the dozens of tiny bird tattoos flying all the way up her right arm to her shoulder.

She had a book in her hand but she put it down as we came in, looked up and smiled.

"Hi, Shell," she said. "Do you need more incense?"

"Yes, have you got any of the myrrh left?"

"Over there." The girl pointed with her book to the far end of the shop.

"Thanks. Oh, this is my friend, Emma, by the way," Shell said, gesturing over her shoulder at me. "Emma, this is Kara. Her mum owns the shop."

"Hello," Kara said to me as I wheeled cautiously

through the narrow aisle. "I like your Joan the Wad amulet."

"Oh, thanks." My hand went to it automatically. "I like your tattoo. What kind of bird are they?"

Now that I was closer I could see that they weren't entirely black as I had first thought but all had a small splash of white above their tail feather – just like the birds in the big oil painting back at the Waterwitch.

"Storm petrels," Kara replied. "They're seabirds. During storms they seek shelter on ships at sea. That's how they got their name."

"Sailors used to think that storm petrels were the spirits of drowned sailors," Shell said, joining us at the till. "Kara is a green witch. She uses nature to work her magic."

"Oh. That's cool," I said, not knowing what else to say.

"Emma doesn't believe in witches," Shell told Kara.

"I never said that," I protested. "I'm trying to be open-minded." I looked at Shell and said, "So do you think that's what you are, too? A green witch?"

"No," she replied. "I'm not like Kara. There are

lots of different kinds of witches, you know. If Mum were alive she could probably explain it to me. But she's not so I just have to figure it out on my own. I don't quite know what I am yet."

"I've been thinking about that," Kara said. "You're obviously not an ordinary white witch – there's a little bit of darkness there, too, something I've never seen before. Maybe you're a pellar."

"What's that?" I asked.

"It comes from the word 'repeller' – as in 'repeller of evil'," Kara said. "Pellars can lift curses, counteract black magic, reverse the effects of ill-wishing, and exorcize demons, dark witches and evil spirits. They're one of the most powerful kinds of witches there is but their magic can be … oh, how can I explain it? Look, whenever I perform magic, I get this tingling feeling in my fingertips," she said. "But a pellar's magic – well, it's a little bit raw, a little bit violent. It's the kind of magic that makes your hands bleed."

I didn't like the sound of that very much so I was glad when Shell shook her head. "I'm not a pellar. If I had magic like that then I would've been able to dispel the birds by now." She pushed a bundle of incense across the counter. "I'll take this, please."

Kara picked up the incense and I noticed she had long acrylic nails that had been painted silver and midnight blue to represent the changing phases of the moon. "Is the witch still in the cellar?" she asked.

Shell nodded. "I hear her most nights."

Kara took the money from Shell, put the incense into a striped paper bag and handed it over. "My offer still stands, you know," she said. "Any time you want me to come and bless the Waterwitch, I'd be more than happy."

"The witch wouldn't like that," Shell said, picking up the bag. "I don't think it would be safe for you."

Kara laughed. "Don't worry about that," she said. "Besides, didn't you say once that it was mostly men she doesn't like?"

I looked at Shell, who shrugged and said, "Well, that's just a feeling I get from her sometimes but I don't know for sure. And, anyway, if you got in her way I don't think it would matter much whether you're a—"

"Shell, honestly, I've blessed countless haunted inns – the Dolphin, the Three Pilchards, the—"

"Yes, but this is a witch's ghost," Shell said.

"It's different. She's different. She can do things that other ghosts can't do."

"Ghosts can't hurt you," Kara said firmly. "They're just wraiths. Hardly more substantial than sea mist."

She glanced towards the door as she spoke and I followed her gaze to see Bailey looking wet, bedraggled and very sorry for himself. He was too well behaved to paw at the door but he was peering in at me through the glass with a woebegone expression on his face and his tail tucked between his legs.

"I'd better get back out to my dog," I said. "I don't want him to get too cold. Nice to meet you."

"And you," Kara replied.

Shell said goodbye, too, and followed me out of the shop. We cut around through Buller Quay where the netting day boats and deep-sea trawlers were moored alongside the fish market, straining against their salt-crusted ropes on the restless grey ocean. The market was shut up now but I used to come here early in the morning with Gran to buy freshly landed seafood for the Waterwitch's restaurant. I still remembered the cases of fish – monk and cuttle, cod and dover, sole and squid, packed in ice in their plastic crates alongside metal traps filled with lobsters and brown crabs, and ceramic pots overflowing with Cornish shellfish and Fowey mussels. Even when the market was shut up and deserted, the smell of seafood never quite left the place.

A few minutes later, Shell, Bailey and I were wedged into a small table in a corner of the Smugglers Bay Inn, a building perched right on the quayside, looking out across the water. We ordered burgers which came with a huge pile of hot chips.

Shell was delighted. "This is the best meal I've had in ages."

She didn't say another word until she'd cleared her plate, even mopping up the grease with her last chip.

"So are you going to tell me about this woman who's been using your hairbrush?" I asked once she'd finished. "The one you were talking to Kara about?"

Shell sighed. "You won't believe me, Emma. No one ever does. But there's a woman down in the cellar of the Waterwitch. I think she came out of that witch bottle we broke. She must be the witch

165

that Christian Slade had put to death. She was on board the *Waterwitch* and now she's here."

"So … do you think she's evil then, if you believe she cursed the ship?"

Shell looked at me for a long time and I got the impression she was trying to decide whether to reply at all when, finally, she said, "She's not evil. It's worse than that. She's mad."

"Mad?"

"Yes, mad. Stark raving. Because of what they did to her, I suppose. I think there must have been fire involved because I smelled burnt flesh coming out of the cellar once. She was probably burned at the stake. That happened a lot to witches back then. I wish there was something I could do to help her." She glanced at me and said, "This probably won't make any sense to you, but I feel a kind of connection with her. Maybe it's because she's another witch. Maybe because I was there when you and Jem broke the bottle. Or maybe because Christian Slade was a relative of mine, which almost makes me feel responsible, in a way, if she's the woman he had killed. And maybe if I help her, she'll help me back by telling me how to get rid of the birds. She's the only person in the world who might know what I'm supposed to do. Even Kara had no idea about the birds when I asked her. But the witch would understand, I know she would."

I tapped my fingers thoughtfully along the wooden table for a moment, thinking about the witch bottle and how it might be connected to Christian Slade's ghost ship.

"They're all over your wheelchair, by the way," Shell continued. "The birds, I mean. They've been there since we came in."

I couldn't help looking round at the back of the chair – and some part of me almost expected to see a row of silent birds staring at me from the handles but, of course, there was nothing.

"Can you lean forward a bit?" Shell asked. "One of them has got stuck. It's making an awful racket."

Against my better judgement, I did as she asked – although the small movement instantly sent a jolt of pain through my back.

"Thanks," Shell said. "I couldn't take much more of that squawking."

When we'd been kids I'd always kind of assumed that Shell's bird thing was just a cry for attention.

Now I wasn't so sure. *Was* it an act or did she really, actually believe we were sitting here surrounded by her strange, mysterious, silent birds?

It felt like there was a noose slowly tightening around my throat. This was not what I had come to Cornwall for. Phantom birds, and ghosts in the cellar, and paintings that moved, and mad women brushing their hair with other people's brushes, and God knows what else. I must be out of my mind to be having this conversation with Shell at all. Jem would be pissed off if he knew. I was supposed to be reassuring Shell that there were no ghosts, not encouraging all her ideas about them.

And yet, Gran seemed to believe that the Waterwitch was haunted. And that man at the museum had told me about his friend who had checked out in the middle of the night. I knew that other guests at the inn had done the same. All those stories had to have started somewhere. They couldn't have just come to life out of nothing.

Suddenly, I recalled the feeling of the witch bottle slicing into my palm as it broke, all those years ago. If there really had been a spirit trapped inside, then I was the one who had let her out...

"Have you tried to find out who she was?" I asked. "The witch, I mean."

"I wouldn't know where to start, Emma. I don't even know her name."

"What about Christian Slade?" I asked.

"What about him?"

"Well, if he's right there in Room 7, like you say, then why don't you just ask *him* about the witch?"

Shell's eyes went very wide and her voice was practically a whisper as she said, "Christian … Christian doesn't speak."

I sighed. "What about the Guildhall Museum then? Doesn't it still have all those old documents and family history stuff? Christian Slade was from Looe originally so they might have some information about him. Why don't we take a look on the way back?"

"Really?"

"Why not?"

We paid the bill and went outside. The rain had stopped but the sea mist still hung about in ribbons that reminded me of shredded sails. It didn't take long to go down the road to where the fifteenth-century Guildhall Museum and Gaol stood on Higher Market Street. Visitors were supposed to enter by way of the outer staircase that led to the first floor so Bailey and I had to wait outside while Shell went and found someone to let us in at ground level. She told them she was doing a school project about the *Waterwitch* and the elderly female volunteer set about helping us to run a search for Christian Slade. They had records of heaps of old documents on microfiche: Parish Registers and census listings, ancient deeds and wills, as well as hundreds and hundreds of old photographs.

"There isn't much that goes back as far as you want, I'm afraid," the volunteer said. "In fact, there are only two mentions of Christian Slade on our database."

The first turned out to be a copy of his will. He had left everything to his wife, Elizabeth Slade, except for the *Waterwitch*. The ship had been left in trust for someone called Annis Slade Merrick.

"That's the first owner of the Waterwitch Inn," Shell explained. "Our great-great-great-something grandmother. I remember Mum telling me about her. It's her side of the family that links us to Christian Slade. Was Annis Merrick his daughter? It's weird that they don't have the same name."

"There's no record of the Slades having any children," the volunteer replied. "But this probably was a child if the ship was left in trust. And there must be some connection as her second name is Slade."

"The will is dated just a couple of weeks before his death," I said. "Almost like he knew he was going to die."

"No one can predict getting crushed by a falling beam, dear," the volunteer said.

"But he'd had poor health, hadn't he?" I asked, remembering what Gran had said years ago. "And he was worried about being cursed."

"He was supposed to have had some kind of nervous breakdown while the *Waterwitch* was being built," the volunteer agreed. "But he must have recovered from that if he went to Dartford to inspect the ship."

"How many other ships had his company built?" I asked.

We looked through some of the shipbuilding records but the *Waterwitch* was the only one listed to Christian's company. It looked as if it was the first and last ship he ever constructed.

"That's strange," the volunteer said. "The second

mention of his name on our database is on these ship plans for another vessel called the *Elizabeth*."

She pulled them up and we all gathered closer around the computer to look at them.

"But that ship is the *Waterwitch*," Shell said at once. "It's identical in every way."

It did seem so, for this too was a 140-foot long, three-masted, 400-ton galleon. But then I noticed the figurehead.

"The figurehead in these plans is a blonde woman," I said. "Whereas the *Waterwitch* figurehead is dark-haired." I frowned. "Wasn't Christian Slade supposed to have been having some kind of argument about the figurehead when he was killed?"

"This ship could have been one he planned to build afterwards," the volunteer said. "In honour of his wife, perhaps?"

"But look at this." I pointed at the date scratched into the plans. "It's the same year the *Waterwitch* was built. That ship *is* the *Waterwitch* except for the different figurehead."

"It ended up with the wrong name," Shell said.

"Perhaps you're right," the volunteer said. She peered closer at the plan and said, "I suppose there's no way to know for sure. Perhaps one of the crew thought the orders to put a witch bottle on board was funny and decided to play a practical joke with the name change?"

"No one would have found it funny," Shell replied. "Everyone believed in witches back then. None of the workers would ever have played a joke like that."

"How else could it have happened, though?" the volunteer said. "A ship's name doesn't just change by magic."

She smiled as she said it but the word *magic* seemed to hang in the air between us. There were no more documents about either Christian Slade or the *Waterwitch* so we thanked the volunteer and left the museum.

"I should be heading off anyway," I said. "I promised Gran I'd visit her again this afternoon. I'll see you back at the Waterwitch, OK?"

We had only just stepped outside when my phone rang. It was Gran's hospice. It turned out that I wasn't going to be visiting her that afternoon after all. In fact, it was too late to visit her ever again. I would never get the chance to ask her about the keys that Jem had received in the post, or any more questions about the Waterwitch. I'd never hug her or feel her hand clasped around mine. She had died an hour ago.

Chapter Twenty-Three

Emma

I knew it was coming, but that didn't help much. Why should it? A punch in the face isn't going to hurt less just because you know it's coming. I would never see Gran again and my memories of her would fade, bit by bit, until I couldn't quite recall the exact sound of her voice, or the way she had looked when she smiled.

There was nothing else to do but go back to the Waterwitch. We stopped at the supermarket on the way and bought some food. I gave Bailey the bread to carry, since that was the lightest bag, and Shell and I carried the rest. Jem was already at the inn when we arrived and when Shell told him about Gran, he squeezed my shoulder and said, "I'm so sorry, Emma."

I wanted to put my hand over his so that he'd leave it there, but I couldn't pluck up the nerve, and in another moment he'd removed it.

175

I went to my room to phone Mum. When I told her about Gran, she went completely silent on the other end of the line. Finally, she said she'd phone the hospice to discuss funeral arrangements, and then asked if I'd be coming home now. I couldn't go back on my promise to keep Shell company so I made up some excuse about wanting to visit some of my old favourite places here in Looe and told her I was still going to stay in Cornwall until the end of half-term.

After hanging up I joined the others in the library where we spent most of the afternoon around the wood-burning stove, playing cards or talking. Jem left at six to start his evening shift at the Seagull, and Shell cooked us the frozen pizzas I'd bought earlier. I didn't have much appetite for mine, and turned my attention instead to the books lining the shelves. After finishing her dinner, Shell went upstairs "to practise with her witch balls" – whatever that meant – and I stayed by the fire, leafing through the books. The shipwreck museum had said that the *Waterwitch* had been built in 1577 so I looked up some of the witches and witchcraft stories from around that time. Like Shell had said, many of the women accused of witchcraft back then had been killed in horrible ways and there was nothing that drew my attention to any one particular woman. Their stories all seemed fairly similar – accused of witchcraft, dragged from their homes, burned at the stake. Sometimes they were drowned or stoned instead.

Shell came down a little later to say that she was tired and going to bed and, as Jem wouldn't be back until gone 1 a.m., I decided to do the same.

As soon as I got back to my bedroom I felt tears pricking my eyes. It wasn't just the fact that Gran was gone, it was all the time I'd wasted with her, too. I sat for a while and cried quietly, which confused and worried Bailey, who poked his snout at me a couple of times before laying his head in my lap. Finally I made myself stop and gave him a scratch behind the ears.

"It's all right, Bailey, I'm OK," I said.

He wagged his tail and flicked his tongue out at my fingers. I was so glad he was here with me and wrapped my arms around him to kiss the top of his head. Then I wheeled across the room to draw the curtains. Remembering what Shell had said earlier about the moon, I looked out for it. I'd seen it earlier from the window of the library and it had very definitely been a crescent moon. I didn't know what I would do if I looked now and saw it was full. But, in fact, I couldn't see the moon at all because the sky had clouded over, hiding even the stars from view.

On a whim, I switched on my iPad to have a look at some of the online reviews. Gran and Shell had both mentioned guests leaving negative reviews online but I hadn't expected there to be quite so many. And hardly any of them were complaining about the food or the staff or the facilities. They were complaining about ghosts.

This seemed odd because, when I looked at reviews for Cornwall's other famous haunted inns, like the Jamaica Inn, there were no complaints about ghostly goings-on. If anything, people seemed to treat the idea of those places really being haunted as a joke or a bit of a novelty. It wasn't like that with the Waterwitch. Some of the guests seemed genuinely frightened.

I'd only scrolled through a few reviews before I found Room 7 mentioned. The guest said he had woken in the middle of the night with blood dripping on to his face from above, and that when he turned on the lights he'd seen actual blood bubbling up through the holes and cracks in the wooden ceiling beam. The review had been written a few months ago by the priest Shell had told me about. He said in the review that he had blessed the room before he left the inn.

Another reviewer claimed that they had taken photos of the Waterwitch from outside and, when they had looked at them later, they'd seen the pale faces of ghostly sailors peering out of the windows. They'd even uploaded one of the photos. One of the windows looked a *little* bit like it had faces in it but the photo was so blurred and grainy that it was impossible to tell for sure. And even if they were faces, it was probably just other guests looking out. The reviewer claimed there'd been no one there at the time but perhaps she had just failed to see them. That was the most likely explanation, after all.

Further on down the page, one inventive reviewer had written: "Those of us who have worked at sea know that ships have souls. It's a matter of historical fact that men were murdered on board the *Waterwitch* and, obviously, the wood remembers."

The wood remembers…

I raised an eyebrow. "Obviously," I muttered.

"Sure. Why shouldn't the wood remember?"

I snapped my iPad cover closed and put it to one side with a sigh. All of a sudden I felt like I couldn't really be bothered with any of this. There were no ghosts – only stories and superstitions. Gran was dead and she was the reason I'd come here in the first place. It would be so nice to just pack up my stuff in the morning and drive home. But I'd promised Jem I'd stick around for half-term to keep Shell company and I couldn't go back on that now. Just a few more days, I told myself.

I was about to start the long process of getting ready for bed when there was a thump at my door. "It's open," I called, thinking it must be Shell wanting something.

But there was no answer so I wheeled myself across the room and pulled the door open on to the dark corridor. There was nobody there, but a single witch ball rested in my doorway, a dark blue sphere of glass. It was one of the larger ones – almost as big as a bowling ball.

"Shell?" I called. I squinted into the darkness. There were no lights on and it was impossible to tell whether there was anyone out there or not. And yet

… I had the definite feeling that there *was* someone in the corridor, watching me. And that feeling became ten times stronger when Bailey joined me in the doorway and instantly started to growl.

"Is anyone there?" I called out, and then felt annoyed with myself for the tremor I heard in my voice.

Silence. I swallowed hard. If we'd been at home I could have simply told Bailey to turn the lights on but I didn't know where they were here, and neither did he. The blackness spilled out towards us like fingers.

I fumbled in my pocket for my phone and flicked on its torch. It was a feeble little beam but I swept it up and down the wall anyway, looking for the light switch. Once the corridor was lit I would be able to see that there was no one there. Or that it was Shell, perhaps, playing some odd kind of joke on me.

But I couldn't see a switch. It was probably further along the corridor but there was no way I was wheeling myself into that blackness, closer to the cellar door and the monster staircase, not if I couldn't see where I was going and what was in front of me.

I was about to turn the chair back into my room when Bailey stopped growling and barked instead

– his ferocious bark that he saved for things he perceived as threats. And then he was squeezing through the gap in the doorway and I knew what he was about to do. I lunged for his collar, wrenching my back in the process, but he was too quick and, the next second, he'd run off into the blackness.

"Bailey!" I called after him. "Come here!"

But he didn't come back. I could hear him at the end of the corridor, barking at something.

And then the barking abruptly stopped.

"Shit! Bailey!" I called again. "Bailey!"

He still didn't come, and those silent shadows almost seemed to sneer at me. Why wasn't Bailey barking? Why wasn't he coming back? I was torn between feeling angry with him and feeling worried. And a little bit scared. Bailey always came when I called him.

I put the phone in my lap to wheel myself over the threshold, into the corridor. It felt like I was propelling myself forwards into total, inky blackness – the kind of impenetrable darkness you might find deep underneath the sea. My wheels seemed to creak excruciatingly loudly on the wooden floorboards as I inched my way further and further down the corridor.

I stopped and held the phone up again, shining the torch around, desperate to find a light switch. It was probably over by the restaurant door, right at the end of the corridor, opposite the staircase. Silently, I cursed Bailey for making me go after him. The whole thing was nuts. A disabled girl in a wheelchair trying to rescue a German Shepherd. It was ridiculous. He was probably fine. I should just leave him to it and go back to bed. But I couldn't take that chance that he might *not* be fine. And Bailey always came back when I called him…

I was just about to continue on down the corridor when my wheelchair started to move all by itself. I heard the soft creak of the wheels and felt cool air brushing against my face as I rolled slowly forwards.

There was someone behind me.

And they were pushing me along.

Chapter Twenty-Four
Jem

My shift was going fine until Dad arrived. I knew this would happen at some point; it was inevitable. Looe was a tiny village and if he wanted to find me then it was just a case of asking in one of the local pubs. And he frequented those regularly enough.

The last time I'd seen him was at the hospital. Shell had texted me to say they were heading there so I left straight from work and arrived before them. I saw Dad's car pull up to the drop-off bay. He wasn't going to even bother to come in with her. That was the thing that made me maddest of all. If I hadn't got there first, she would have been completely alone. As soon as Shell saw me, she practically flew out of the car. I'd been afraid that there might be bruises on her face, or a cut lip, or a black eye. That, at least, wasn't the case. It was only the arm. But that was more than enough.

"It's OK," I said, even though – plainly – it wasn't

OK at all. "Go in, I'm right behind you."

She glanced over her shoulder at me, but did as I'd said and went into the hospital. Since I'd made no move to do it, Dad reached across and slammed the passenger door closed. Vaguely, I noticed that he had a nasty-looking cut just beneath his right eye, and I wondered for a moment if Shell could have done it with her nails, but it looked too deep for that. I guess he would have just driven off without a word if I hadn't stepped out in front of the car, forcing him to slam on the brakes.

I smashed my fist down hard on the bonnet and there was a savage kind of satisfaction in feeling the metal crunch beneath my hand. Then I moved round to the driver's door and pulled it open. I had never hit Dad before in my life, never hit anyone, in fact, but, in that moment, my arm ached to throw a punch, and it must have shown on my face because Dad shrank back from me.

"We are never coming back," I said, slowly and clearly. I had never meant anything more in my entire life.

Dad didn't reply. He just slammed the door shut. I think he'd hoped to catch my fingers but I pulled them away too quickly and, the next moment, he was driving off, and I knew that was the end of it, the end of the three of us ever again trying to live together like a normal family. Emma's gran had sent me the keys for the Waterwitch that very day, so at least we had somewhere to go.

Shell and I went back to the cottage that night when we knew he'd be at work on the boats. I got the suitcases out of the loft, packed up my stuff and told Shell to do the same – to take everything with her that she didn't want to leave behind. That was a mistake, I guess. I should have helped her pack. When we got to the Waterwitch I discovered that her suitcase was full of witch balls – and nothing else. She'd brought no clothes, no toiletries, nothing. When I went back to the cottage by myself the next night to collect the rest of her things, I found that Dad had changed the locks. It was a petty act of spite that didn't surprise me at all. It was just the way I would have expected him to behave.

But I knew, at some point, he would resent the fact that I'd taken Shell away. And he would miss the money I used to bring in. And then he would come after me.

Today, I didn't need anyone to tell me he was there – I heard him from the kitchen – that familiar shout of rage that seemed to be his default setting.

"*Where is that selfish little shit?*"

I almost dropped the plate I'd just picked up.

God, no, I thought. *Not at work. Anywhere but here.*

"Hey, Jem, you're not going to believe this," Sam said, coming into the kitchen. "There's some drunk dude in the restaurant going crazy. Do you think we should call the police?"

"No," I said. "I'll deal with it."

"Mate, seriously, that guy is enormous! I really don't think you want to—"

"I'll deal with it. He's my father."

Sam's mouth dropped open in shock and I was reminded of the look Ben had given me all those years ago as we sat together at the kitchen table, listening to those terrible slow slaps.

I went past him and pushed open the door to the restaurant. All the guests had gone silent. The Seagull was a nice, upmarket guest house. A drunken fisherman bursting in and screaming the place down was not the kind of thing these people would be accustomed to.

187

Dad stood in the middle of the room, wearing his filthy fisherman's overalls. Blood and grease and fish guts were smeared across the front, and his black lace-up boots were crusted with salt. Sam was right about him being enormous – not with fat but with muscle. Dad had worked as a fisherman since he was fifteen years old and a lifetime of hauling traps and dragging nets and lifting crates would make anyone strong.

"So this is where you've been slinking around!" Dad said, pointing an unsteady finger at me across the room, his upper lip curling in a snarl.

I walked towards him but it felt like I was moving through water, hot water that boiled and bubbled around me. This was the kind of thing that gave the Penhales a bad name, and caused people to whisper about us, and generally think that the whole damn lot of us were rotten to the core.

"You owe me money!" Dad said. "And I'm sure as hell not leaving without it."

"Talk to me about it outside," I said.

"I'll talk to you about it wherever I damn well like!"

He lunged at me, but drink had made him slow and I was easily able to duck out of his reach. With nothing to grab on to, Dad's momentum carried him forwards and he crashed on top of a nearby table. Cutlery went everywhere, glasses toppled over and smashed, Dad lost his balance and went down, dragging the entire tablecloth with him. Unluckily, I had just delivered main courses to that table, and he ended up covered in shrimps and linguini.

Behind me, I heard someone laugh. It was a nervous kind of laugh, but it was a laugh just the same, and I knew I had to act quickly because Dad couldn't stand to be laughed at. I had seen him attack perfect strangers before when he was drunk, and I knew he'd do it again if the mood took him.

I grabbed his arm and somehow managed to haul him to his feet, although all the muscles in my arms and back felt like they were on fire. Stumbling blindly, I managed to half drag, half carry him across the room and out of the door to the street.

But, even drunk, he was stronger than me, and I couldn't prevent him from twisting in my grip, grabbing my shoulders and then hurling his full body weight at me. He probably intended for us to go crashing to the ground but I managed to stay upright as I staggered back, which didn't really help matters because then I hit the wall instead and the back of my head struck the stone so hard that, for a white, bright moment, I couldn't see anything at all.

"You selfish little arsehole!" Dad roared in my face, the sour stink of alcohol strong on his breath. "I looked after the pair of you for years – fed you, clothed you, the works – and the first chance you get you stab me in the back!"

"No one is stabbing you in the back," I managed, willing the flashing lights to fade from my vision. "You know why we had to leave."

His fingers were digging hard into my shoulders, like he wanted to bruise the bone. It was bad, very bad, to be pinned up against the wall like this.

"You know what it's like in October." Dad spat the words at me. "Half the time the weather's too rough to take the boats out. And if we can't take the boats out then we can't earn any money. I've had no food in the house since yesterday!"

I curled my foot around Dad's ankle and yanked sharply. It wasn't enough to make him fall, but it distracted him so that I could duck out from beneath his grip.

"Let's get one thing straight," I said, moving back

to a safe distance. "I'm not giving you any money, not a penny! We have nothing to spare."

"Always thinking of yourself first! Why am I even surprised?"

He took a few unsteady steps towards me but he was swaying on his feet and it was easy enough to stay out of his reach now that there was more room. I guessed that the cold air had hit him, too. I looked again at his overalls, shook my head and said, "You're not working tonight, are you?"

"Course I am — didn't you hear what I just said? Practically no work this month but the boats are going out tonight and I'm going to be on them."

"Dad, you can't drive like this," I said.

He'd worked on a mackerel boat going out from Looe until they'd fired him — he never told us what for, but I guessed it was probably for being drunk on board, or maybe punching the captain, or missing the boat. Dad took it as further evidence that the whole world was out to get him, that he'd been stabbed in the back again, that no one in his life was worth knowing or trusting. Now he fished lobsters and brown crabs on a fishing boat moored at Fowey, a forty-minute drive away.

Dad glared at me with bloodshot eyes. "Don't you tell me what to do." He spoke quietly, which was almost worse than the shouting. "Don't you *ever* tell me what to do."

Then, all of a sudden, he bent over double and vomited into the street. I glanced at the Seagull and saw curious faces pressed up against the glass, staring out at us, mesmerized by this show we were putting on for them.

Once he'd finished, Dad just sort of folded up on the spot and sat slumped on the cobbles, wiping strings of vomit away from his face with the back of his hand. My head throbbed from the force of the impact with the wall and I felt something warm creeping down the back of my neck. I raised my hand to run my fingers over it and they came away smeared with blood. Bizarrely, I was suddenly reminded of finger-painting with Dad one day when I'd been really small. Mum had brought us egg cups filled with chocolate drops. It had been one of the good days.

Part of me was screaming that I should just walk away and leave Dad in the street, just leave him to take his chances and make his mistakes, but some other tiny part of me ached at the sight of him slumped there like that.

In her own way, Mum had not been an easy person to live with. And Shell could be odd, too, with her witch balls and her birds, but that didn't excuse the things Dad had done. It didn't excuse the bruises and blood and broken bones. Nothing could.

It would have been simpler if there had never been any good times at all. If Dad could have been awful to us all the time, that would have made it easier in a perverse kind of way. Easier to leave for good, to cut ties, to never have anything to do with him ever again. I wished I could believe that he was evil through and through. I wished I didn't remember the finger-painting, or the day he took me crabbing, or that time he came to my school play and sat in the front row and clapped and clapped with everyone else, and actually looked proud, and didn't once shout or swear or punch anyone.

If I could only hate him then this would be easy; it was loving him that made it so unbearable.

"Even if I wanted to, I've got no spare money to give you," I said quietly. "You can believe me or not but it's the truth."

I stepped forward and, in his current state, it was simple enough to slip my hand into Dad's pocket and whip out his car keys. "I'm going to put these behind the bar," I said. "You can come back for them in the morning. If your mind is set about going to work then do yourself a favour and go and get some coffee or something. Try to sober up. Then get a taxi. You can't drive to Fowey like this. You'll kill yourself. Or someone else."

I turned to walk away from him. But then he said thickly behind me, "How am I s'posed to get a taxi with no money, Jem?"

He hardly ever called me by my name and it felt like a giant fist squeezing around my heart.

Just leave! The voice inside my head screamed. *It's not your problem. Just leave, just leave, just—*

"Here," I said, holding the note out to him. It was like I'd taken it from my pocket without even realizing it. "This should cover the taxi."

Dad snatched it from me with a grunt.

"Don't try to find Shell," I said. "If you see her in the street, don't speak to her. She doesn't have any money. And she's never coming back to live with you."

Dad looked up, his bloodshot eyes squinting at me

in the dark. "Live with me?" he said, croaking out the words. "*Live with me?* Are you kidding? I would never have that psycho back in the house again. Not after what she did."

I stared at him, the blood pounding and pounding in my ears. "What *she* did?" I repeated. "God, Dad." I ran both hands through my hair, resisting the urge to grab great fistfuls and start pulling it out. How were you supposed to communicate with someone who always twisted things around so that no matter what they did or said, no matter who they hurt or how despicably they behaved, in their own minds they were never to blame?

"*You* broke *her* arm!" I burst out at last.

Dad scrambled to his feet and suddenly he was towering over me again in the road. "Didn't she tell you what happened?" he asked, leaning closer. "Didn't you ever ask her?"

"I didn't need to," I replied, refusing to step back this time. "I know what happened. I can imagine it easily enough. Christ, hasn't the same thing happened to me a thousand times?"

Dad did something then that astonished me – he laughed. Then he laughed some more. "You think you're so noble, don't you?" He reached out and shoved me hard enough to make me stagger back a couple of steps. "The hero of the hour," he snarled, "protecting his poor defenceless sister from their drunken brute of a father. You said to me once that I twist everything up in my head to come up with a reality that suits me – well, guess what? You do exactly the same thing! It's easy to blame me for everything, isn't it? But you just ask her! Ask her why I broke her arm. I wouldn't have that girl back in the house for anything, do you hear me? Not for anything! Why do you think I changed the locks? And if you've got any sense at all in that thick head of yours, you'll drop her off at the nearest mental hospital and you'll never look back. Cut her loose, maybe you'll have some kind of a chance then. That girl is cracked. Her mother saw to that."

I turned away from him, disgusted. "I don't believe a word you're saying."

Dad didn't reply, he just laughed again, and I left him like that – drunk and laughing in the street.

Chapter Twenty-Five
Emma

I could feel the scream bubbling up in my chest and it took every scrap of willpower I had to suppress it. There was someone behind me in the dark, and I couldn't see them but I knew they were there because my wheelchair was rolling briskly along the smooth wooden floorboards, and wasn't that the click of footsteps I could hear? And the smell – just the faintest smell of burning flesh...

"Who's there?" I cried out, twisting painfully in my seat to sweep my arms blindly behind me, trying to touch whoever it was, to grab their wrists and make them stop, but my hands only brushed air.

I reached out to the wall to stop the momentum and, by chance, my hands finally found the light switch. The darkness disappeared and sickly light from the wall sconces filled the corridor, illuminating the cellar door and the nearby monster staircase. I looked over my shoulder, filled with dread as to what I might see standing there behind me…

But there was no one.

Nobody behind me, nobody pushing the chair, nobody else in the entire corridor. Just an empty space stretching back to my room. The next second I realized why my chair had been moving by itself. It was the most obvious explanation, the one I should have thought of straight away: the corridor was on a slight slope.

And yet … I didn't remember noticing that before when I went to my room. Normally, even the smallest slope was painfully obvious when you were wheeling yourself up it. Above my head, some old part of the building groaned softly but, somehow, it sounded more like the groan of a ship sinking than a building settling.

I told myself to stop being such a total idiot. Then I looked up at the corridor in front of me again and I knew – I *knew* – that it was just in my imagination but, honest to God, the corridor looked just a little bit more sloped than it had a moment before.

As if on cue, my wheelchair started sliding forwards again but, this time, I let it happen. From where I was sitting I could see that the restaurant door was open, even though I could have sworn I'd closed it earlier. Bailey must have gone through there. Perhaps he was out of earshot and that was why he hadn't come back. As I reached the end of the corridor, I noticed that all the paintings hanging on the wall were tilting sharply to the left. What the hell was going on here?

Under the watchful gaze of the many staring eyes of the monster staircase, I turned my wheelchair into the restaurant and snapped on the light. My eyes were drawn instantly to the *Waterwitch* painting above the fireplace and, just for the briefest moment, it really looked as if the deck of the ship wasn't empty but full of row upon row of sailors, all staring straight out of the canvas at me. Then I blinked and they were gone, they had never been there at all, it was just an empty deck and a deserted ghost ship, pale hands reaching out of the water below as the crew drowned in the dark.

"Bailey!" I called, but my voice came out a weird, strangled half-whisper. I cleared my throat and tried again. "Bailey!"

I scanned the restaurant, trying to see everything all at once, but it was difficult when the place was so full of nooks and crannies. I almost jumped out of my skin when my dog came bursting out from beneath a table.

"God, Bailey!" I said, gasping for breath. "You scared the crap out of me!"

He was totally hyper, running around and around in circles the way he did whenever he was really excited about something, and he was panting so hard that his tongue was hanging down out of his mouth and dripping drool.

"It's OK, you daft mutt," I said, leaning forward to soothe him as he frantically tried to lick my face. "Come on. I think that's enough drama for one night. Let's go back to bed."

We left the restaurant together and went back out into the corridor. And the strangest thing was that, as I wheeled myself back to my room, the floor no longer seemed to be tilting at all. In fact, it seemed completely and perfectly flat. Flat as a damn pancake.

Chapter Twenty-Six

Shell

The birds woke me in the early hours of the morning.

It wasn't yet 6 a.m. and still completely dark outside. I tried to push them away and pull the covers up over my head but the horrible creatures squirmed underneath, their clawed feet tangling in my hair as wings brushed over my face and beaks scratched at my skin. I threw back the covers and stumbled out of bed, dragging the struggling birds from my hair and flinging them to the floor.

Then I hurried out of my room and down the staircase. It was so early that I didn't expect anyone else to be up, but when I approached the library, I saw soft light spilling out of the doorway. I walked in and was startled to see Jem there, fully dressed, sitting in the leather chesterfield armchair beneath the huge wooden *Waterwitch* light hanging from the ceiling. He wasn't doing anything. Just staring straight ahead at the cold grate of the wood-burning stove. The sickly glow from the ship wasn't enough to light the large room properly so he had turned on a couple of the table lamps, but shadows still danced in the corners.

"What are you doing up so early?" I asked.

Jem jumped at my voice, and turned his head towards me. The dark circles beneath his eyes were even more pronounced than usual. He looked terrible. I was vaguely aware that the birds had followed me into the room, their claws skittering over the wooden floorboards, but they weren't pecking at me any more so I ignored them.

"Couldn't sleep," Jem said. "What are you doing up?"

I shrugged. "I couldn't sleep, either."

"Shell..." Jem said slowly. "I was just thinking. You never told me what happened the day Dad broke your arm."

I was startled to hear him bring the subject up. We didn't talk about things like this. We never had. It was almost a kind of rule of ours. If you didn't speak of it, then you could pretend it didn't really happen.

"I made him angry," I said.

"Yes, but *how* did you make him angry?"

"It wasn't me, really, it was the birds." I looked

at them gathered around my feet, pecking at the floorboards.

"The birds," Jem repeated in a flat voice. "Right. What did the birds do then?"

"They ... they..." I swallowed hard. "One of them tried to peck Dad's eye out."

A strange look came over my brother's face. "What do you mean by that exactly?"

"I was making dinner and Dad got angry because it was late. He came into the kitchen and started shouting – you know – like he does sometimes, at ... at the top of his voice."

Jem nodded. "Yes," he said. "I know. Go on."

"And I think ... I think the birds don't like loud sounds so they ... they flew at him and one of them was heading straight for his face." I trembled at the memory. "It was going to peck his eye out. So I reached out to grab it but I'd been chopping vegetables and I still had the knife in my hand and I think Dad must've thought I was trying to stab him with it." I shook my head and said, "I was only trying to help him. I was only trying to protect him from the bird. It dug its beak into the skin below his eye – that thin skin where you can see the veins running underneath – and it drew blood. But Dad thought I was responsible. He thought it was me."

Before Jem could reply, the light from the ship model above flickered and there was a buzzing sound as if an internal wire had just come loose. Then, in a shower of plaster, one of the hooks suddenly ripped out of the ceiling. The remaining cords couldn't take the additional weight and their hooks were torn free as well. The lights in the ship went out as the entire thing plummeted downwards, straight towards Jem.

I started forwards but I could see that I would never reach him in time. He was already halfway out of the chair but it wasn't going to be enough. Time stopped and I saw, with total terrifying clarity, that the huge wooden ship was going to smash right on top of him.

But then the air filled with wings and the birds were flying past me and their claws were digging into the back of Jem's T-shirt. They yanked him forwards and he sprawled across the floor at the same moment that the ship landed on the armchair, the prow ripping right through the leather.

I stared at it in horrified silence. If Jem had still been sitting there – if the birds hadn't dragged him out of the way just in time — then he could have been seriously hurt. I hurried forwards to help him up and when he saw what had happened to the armchair he'd been occupying moments before he paled and said, "God, that was … that was lucky. Good thing I tripped."

I looked at the birds ruffling their feathers at our feet and knew that his near miss had nothing to do with luck.

"Are you OK?" I asked.

"Yes, fine." He dusted off his clothes and looked up at the ceiling. "This place needs some proper maintenance work doing to it."

Together, we managed to drag the ship free from the armchair. It was too heavy for us to carry, even between us, so we propped it on the floor beside the chair, and then swept up the pieces of plaster in silence.

"Jem," I said at last, my voice so quiet it was almost a whisper.

"What?"

"Do you think it's my fault Dad broke my arm?"

"Of course I don't," he said, but I noticed he wouldn't look at me. "How can you even ask me that?

Look, just forget it. Let's not ever bring it up again. You're out of there now. It's over."

He went back upstairs then, saying he might try to catch an hour's sleep. For long silent moments after he'd gone, I stared at the birds and the birds stared straight back at me with their bright, shining eyes.

"Why did you do that?" I finally whispered. I'd always thought of the birds as a menacing, malicious presence, troubling me, tormenting me, haunting me. So this – what I had just seen them do, saving Jem – it didn't make sense.

The birds rustled their wings and then they melted back into the shadows and were gone. I turned out the lamps and went back to my room, still feeling shaken. When I got up there I lay down on my bed to think it all over.

Perhaps the birds weren't evil, after all. How could they be when they had saved the life of the person I loved most in the world? But they were no ordinary birds, either. Maybe they were familiars? Mum had had one. A black cat called Smoke. She told me that he wasn't a normal pet, but a cat-shaped spirit sent to help her with her magic.

I could see Smoke, though – everyone could.

From the outside he looked just like a normal house cat. My birds weren't like that. No one else ever saw them. But *were* they trying to haunt me? I didn't know what to think any more.

Finally, I closed my eyes, intending to rest them just for a moment but, before I knew it, I was asleep.

Chapter Twenty-Seven
Shell

I woke up to sunlight streaming in through the windows, lighting up the witch balls and making them beautiful in their baskets, winking all their different colours back at me. I sat up and my thoughts went straight to the birds and what they had done earlier this morning.

I picked up a purple witch ball from the side of my bed and looked at it thoughtfully. I hadn't been entirely truthful when I told Emma I wouldn't know where to start trying to find out about the witch. I'd been looking for her in the witch balls since I first arrived but with no success. I'd seen the *Waterwitch* floating on the surface of the ocean, and lost sailors had appeared in the glass a couple of times – but never the witch herself.

I tried it again now but the birds made it hard to concentrate. I could hear them over in the corner, pecking at the balls in their baskets. Their beaks rang out sharply against the glass and I was afraid they'd shatter them if they kept on like that.

Instead, they upended the basket, and the witch balls went rolling off in every direction. I got up from the bed, walking between the birds in my bare feet, trying to avoid treading on them while scooping up the glass balls. The birds skittered away from me, their claws tapping across the floor, but then, strangely, they all gathered around a single red witch ball.

"You want me to try this one?" I asked, picking it up off the floor.

I took it back to the bed and the birds followed me. It was a deep red, the colour of the sea during a blood-sunset. There were six or seven birds on the bed with me now, all rustling their wings and clicking their beaks in this eager, excited kind of way.

"OK," I whispered, and the shining black beads of their eyes all stared back at me, waiting.

I cupped the witch ball in my left hand and looked into it. At first, all I saw was my own face reflected back in the glass, along with the birds fluttering to and fro behind me. But then there was a shift and I saw something else – something *inside* the red glass sphere. I thought it would probably be another sailor but, this time, the ball showed me something else: a woman sitting on a clifftop during springtime. I knew it was late spring because of the masses of wild coastal flowers in full bloom around her, all along the sea slope. Splashes of yellow and red, great sprays of pink and orange and blue. An entire carpet of ox-eye daisies and rock sea spurry, sea carrot and spring squill spread out all around her, as far as the eye could see. I almost thought I could smell that floral scent, mixed with the salted tang of the ocean roaring in rhythmic whispers below.

The woman was incredibly beautiful, with long, dark hair that tumbled loose down her back, and she wore a simple, cream-coloured dress. She looked familiar somehow, and I wondered if I could have seen her before somewhere when, suddenly, it struck me. She bore an uncanny resemblance to the dark-haired figurehead in the giant oil painting of the *Waterwitch* downstairs, only without any hint of that terrible madness.

I thought she was alone at first but then I realized there was a little girl with her, about three years old. I couldn't hear anything from the witch ball but I could see that the woman and the girl were

210

laughing together as they made flower chains out of egg-yolk-coloured yellow flowers that had to be bird's-foot trefoil. No other flower in the world was as yellow as that.

Then the woman looked up, as if she'd heard something that had startled her, and I saw a look of awful fear come over her face as she got to her feet. A moment later I saw what she had seen – six uniformed men approaching across the clifftop, all carrying muskets.

It was hard to watch the woman being dragged away from her daughter and hard to watch her pleading with the men and hard to watch them shaking their heads at her like they just didn't care. From the way the woman was gesturing at the little girl clinging to her skirt I guessed she was trying to tell them that the child was too small to be taken away from her.

But they pulled them apart anyway and, when the girl tried to get back to her mother, one of the men gave her a backhanded slap that split her lip and left her sprawled amongst the wildflowers. I saw the woman struggling in their grip, screaming and fighting, the yellow petals tumbling down out of her hair. But it was no good, nothing she did made any difference. She was dragged away in one direction, while her daughter was led off in the other, getting further and further away from her...

"Shell? Are you up?"

I jumped as I heard Emma's voice calling me from downstairs and the image in the witch ball vanished.

"Yes," I called back. "I'm up." I shoved the birds aside, ignoring their squawks of protest, and walked out to the end of the staircase. Emma was there at the foot of the stairs, Bailey at her side.

"Do you want some breakfast?" she asked. "We've got toast and—"

"Jem said you can drive," I interrupted. "And that you have a car?"

Emma paused, then said, "Yes. Why? Did you want to go somewhere?"

"Would you take me to Boscastle?"

"What's in Boscastle?"

"The Witchcraft Museum. I... There's something I want to look at there."

"All right. What is it that you want to—"

"Great! I'll just get my coat. Where's Jem?"

"He already left. He said that the Seagull doesn't

have any more work for him so he's going to spend the morning taking his CV to other pubs."

"Oh."

That was bad. We'd thought Jem might get another couple of weeks out of the Seagull before the low season really kicked in.

"No wonder he couldn't sleep last night." I looked back down at Emma and said, "Did he tell you what happened in the library?"

"Yes. That must have been horrible. It's a good thing he managed to get out of the way in time."

"Mmm."

"Shell?" Emma said. "Were you … did you drop a witch ball out here last night?"

I shook my head. "No. Why?"

"There was one on the floor outside my door," she said. "Then Bailey ran out of the room and, by the time I brought him back, the witch ball had gone."

"I told you," I said quietly, "they move around at night sometimes."

"Or perhaps the building moves," Emma said.

"What?"

"Never mind. Let's have breakfast and then I'll go and fetch the car."

Chapter Twenty-Eight

Emma

It was about an hour's drive to Boscastle, on the other side of Bodmin Moor. I'd forgotten what a lonely place it was, with towering granite tors and windswept marshes, pitted and scarred from so many years of mining and quarrying.

I remembered Mum and Dad taking me for a drive to see the Stripple Stones on the south slope of Hawk's Tor once. Of the original twenty-eight stones, only fifteen were left.

"No one really knows for sure what the standing stones were supposed to be for back in the Stone Age," Dad had said. "That's what makes them so interesting."

We didn't pass the Stripple Stones this time but I did spot the Hurlers in the distance when we were about halfway across the moor, tall and morose against the natural granite skyline of the Cheesewring.

Shell and I didn't talk much during the drive but it

wasn't an awkward silence, and soon we had reached the Witchcraft Museum. I knew we were in the right place because of the picture of the broomstick-riding hag outside. There was even a sign warning that children, or people of a nervous disposition, might find some of the exhibits in the museum upsetting.

"Have you been here before?" I asked.

"Once. On a school trip."

"So what was it you wanted to look at this time?"

"I just want to get some ideas."

"For what?"

"For what might have turned the witch mad."

I wasn't sure Jem would approve of this expedition, but I paid our entrance fees and the three of us went in. Like the shipwreck museum in Looe, this was an old stone building, absolutely stuffed with artefacts. We went past cabinets filled with maze stones, witch mirrors, puzzle coffins with beeswax poppet dolls and fortune-telling teacups.

The sea witch section had an ancient pair of bone prickers carefully displayed in a wooden box, and I read that these were one of the tools West Country witches were supposed to use for making sea magic and wind rituals. If fishing boats had no success with their catch, they'd suspect they were victims of a sea witch's curse, and would tie strings of hag stones to the side of the boat to counteract it.

Next, Shell and I turned the corner and came face-to-face with a witch's bridle – a terrible iron muzzle designed to fit over a woman's head and force four sharp prongs into her mouth against the tongue and cheeks. The device prevented the woman from talking so that she couldn't call out and curse her attackers while she was being whipped and paraded naked through the streets. The tongue prong had spikes on it so that the woman would slice her tongue open if she tried to talk. The bridle even had a chain attached, presumably so that the witch could be led about like a dog on a lead, yanked around by a chain while her mouth filled up with blood. When I peered closer at the horrible thing, I could see ancient reddish stains on it.

I guessed this was the section they were talking about when they warned about the museum being unsuitable for kids and nervous people. The bridle was making me pretty nervous myself, and Shell didn't seem to be able to take her eyes off it. I think she would have stood there and stared at it all day if I'd let her. By the time we'd walked past a pair of bone-crushing bootikens, a Pear of Anguish and a Witch's Chair covered in one and a half thousand iron spikes, I was starting to feel a bit sick.

Finally, we reached the section with the witch bottles and stared in at the collection behind the glass. One old bottle was surrounded by the yellow bones, rusty nails and human hair that had been inside it. They all looked quite similar to the one we had found in the fireplace seven years ago. When I read the placard I saw that no one really knew for sure what witch bottles were supposed to be for. Some said they were used as curses, others that they were protective magic and some suggested that the witch bottles were "spirit houses" that could be used to contain an evil spirit.

We were just about to leave the museum when we stopped to look at the wall at the exit. There was a list of names printed there, of the women who had been accused of witchcraft and put to death in Cornwall. Shell spotted it first, tapped me on the arm and pointed wordlessly.

The name Slade was there on the wall, and so was Merrick – the same name belonging to the girl

Christian Slade had provided for in his will.

It was right there: Cordelia Merrick, accused of witchcraft by Christian Slade and put to death in the year 1577 – the exact same year that the *Waterwitch* was built.

Chapter Twenty-Nine

Emma

Shell and I bought some food from a nearby shop to eat in the car and then started the journey back across the moor. I was glad to avoid driving in the dark. Perhaps it was just the low-hanging cloud and mist but people did tend to get lost a lot, even when they were travelling along a road they knew well. I was glad of the Joan the Wad amulet hanging from my neck, too. The Queen of the Piskies would lead us safely home, even if the satnav failed.

We talked about Christian Slade and the woman he had accused of witchcraft, Cordelia Merrick, the whole way back. "He must have had an affair with her," Shell said. "I bet he was the father of her daughter. That's why the girl's second name was Slade. And why he left her the ship in his will."

"You know what that means, though, don't you?" I said. "If you're right about Annis Merrick being Christian and Cordelia's child then it means you and Jem are distantly related to both Christian Slade *and* the witch."

"Mum always said that we came from a long line of witches," Shell replied. "And maybe that's why I've felt a sort of connection to the woman at the Waterwitch. It's not just that she's a witch, it's that she's related to me, too."

"But what do you think went wrong with her and Christian?"

Shell shrugged. "Maybe his wife found out so he exposed her as a witch to get her out of the way?"

"Nice guy," I said.

"*I'd* want to curse someone's ship if they did that to me," Shell said. "Wouldn't you?"

"I guess so."

It was only mid-afternoon by the time we arrived in Looe but the overcast sky meant that many of the buildings had their lights turned on already. Just as I looked at the dark facade of the Waterwitch, the light in the second-floor corridor came on and a shadow passed across the window, as if someone had just walked along there.

Shell saw it, too, and frowned. "We never use the top floor," she said. "It must be her. Wandering around. She does that sometimes."

"It's probably Jem," I replied. "He must be back by now."

"It isn't Jem," Shell replied, and she sounded so sure.

We went into the Waterwitch and found him sitting at the kitchen table staring at a cold mug of tea.

"Were you on the second floor?" Shell asked.

He looked up. "When?"

"Just now."

He shook his head. "I haven't been up there today."

"We just saw a light turn on from outside," I said.

Jem frowned. "I'll go and check."

"Take Bailey with you." My cowardly German Shepherd had picked up his bear and clamped it between his teeth the moment we entered the building so I took it away from him and he gave me a hurt look. "You can have it back in a minute," I promised.

Jem and Bailey went up and returned a moment later. "There was a light on but there was no one there," Jem said. "I checked all the rooms –

there was nothing. Perhaps I switched the light on by mistake from downstairs. Anyway, I just put the kettle on if anyone wants a cup of tea?"

"No thanks," Shell said. She went upstairs without another word. I gave Bailey back his bear and we returned to the kitchen with Jem.

Chapter Thirty

Shell

The birds were waiting for me when I got upstairs. There were so many of them that I could hardly enter the room. I had to push hard against the door to get them to move out of the way, and the entire floor was glossy with black feathers and shiny, shiny wings.

They knew what I wanted and had already picked out a witch ball for me – a black onyx one that sat expectantly on my pillow with the birds clustered around it, looking pleased with themselves. I walked over and the birds cleared a path across the floor for me. I sat down on the bed and picked up the witch ball. It was larger and heavier than the red one I had used this morning so I cradled it in my lap and stared down through the glass to the swirling flecks of silver, right in the centre.

The birds rustled their wings and I let them get closer to me on the bed, their small bodies pressed up against mine, the beat of a tiny hundred hearts keeping rhythm with my own as it sped up inside my chest. I guess I knew I was going to see something bad in the witch ball, but I never thought it would be quite so awful.

The woman – Cordelia Merrick, as I now knew her to be – was there in the glass almost straight away this time. But she wasn't on a clifftop surrounded by flowers. She was on a harbour wall, wearing a dress that was dirty and torn, surrounded by people who were jeering and shouting at her. I could tell it wasn't spring any more because the crowd were all wearing thick cloaks. A bonfire sent great billows of smoke and glowing red sparks out over the grey ocean waves, and a magistrates' bench had been set up close to the pier. I realized that Christian Slade stood alongside it, dark-haired and handsome, dressed in a black cloak fastened at the neck with shining pearl buttons. His boots were polished; his gloves and hat looked soft and warm. His grey eyes were cold, though, and the hard expression in them made me shiver.

Suddenly, Cordelia broke away from the man who'd been holding her, ran straight to Christian and threw her arms around him. But Christian did not return her embrace. Instead, he pushed her away so forcefully that she sprawled on the cobblestones at his feet. Then he looked around at the blonde, beautifully dressed woman standing behind him. I remembered the fair-haired figurehead in the ship plans for the *Elizabeth* and wondered if this woman could be his wife. She gave him a chilly look before turning and walking away through the crowd. Christian tried to follow her but one of the magistrates grabbed his arm and indicated that he should stay. He scowled, reluctantly turning back to witness the scene in front of him.

A couple of men had hauled Cordelia to her feet. She struggled desperately as they dragged her on to the pier, but there were too many of them and only one of her. She looked back at Christian, screaming at him, but he just stared straight ahead with a stony expression.

I thought they were going to throw her into the sea to drown, but, instead, one of the men reached into the flames of the bonfire with a pair of iron gloves and brought out a hideous metal contraption – one that I recognized from the museum earlier.

It was a witch's bridle, glowing and smoking and sparking with red-hot heat.

Cordelia screamed and I saw the expression on Christian's face change. He looked genuinely shocked at the sight of the bridle. More than shocked – appalled. He started arguing with one of the magistrates, but the man only shrugged back at him indifferently.

A wooden block was carried on to the pier and Cordelia was forced on to it, her arms and legs secured with black leather straps while her head hung loose over the end. Seeing this, Christian started forwards, as if to intervene, but one of the magistrates moved to block his way.

Push past him! I was silently screaming at him. *Don't just stand there! Do something!*

But Christian didn't push past him. With one last glance at Cordelia, he set his jaw and turned away, refusing to watch.

The red-hot mask was fastened over Cordelia Merrick's face – a long metal band reached down over her head, split at her nose and formed a solid strip of metal across her lips. I knew that the muzzle would force four prongs into her mouth, to hold down her tongue and press against her cheeks. The device would have worked just as well without being heated in the flames first — it was just one more level of cruelty.

Cordelia jerked and bucked against her leather straps, and I could smell the dreadful scent of burning skin and hair. I bit my lip and forced myself not to look away. Eventually, Cordelia lay limp and lifeless on the wooden block. The men untied the straps holding her down, but then something happened, something changed. The crowd weren't laughing and clapping any more, they were looking worried, they were backing away from the wooden block. And then I heard it, too, faintly at first, but getting louder and louder. It was that demented laugh I had heard before. It was soft and muffled, coming from within the witch ball, but it was definitely the same sound. The woman was lying there with steel spikes piercing her tongue and half her face burnt off, and yet she was laughing, and laughing, and laughing...

She turned her head so that she was looking along the pier towards Christian. Thinking it finished, he had looked back at her again, but then her arm slowly raised to point right at him with a trembling hand.

He blanched and stumbled back a few steps, an expression of utter horror on his white face.

The laughing took on a bubbling sound and I peered closer, dismayed to realize that there was blood seeping out from underneath the mask, trailing down her neck, running on to the wood. The men quickly tied her hands and feet together and, the next moment, she was thrown into the sea to sink beneath the cold, grey surface. Clouds of steam hissed up angrily where the water touched the glowing, hot mask.

Christian was on his knees with his head in his hands as the rest of the crowd surged forwards to catch their last glimpse of the witch. The water closed over her head and then she was gone, leaving nothing behind but the blood running down the grooves in the wooden block. Then it was coming out of the witch ball itself, creeping in thick, sludgy lines down my wrists and arms.

I cried out and dropped the ball, leaped to my feet and watched the sheets turn slick and scarlet, all slippery with clots and platelets, filling the air with the metallic scent of death and dying.

It was so overpowering that I gave a dry heave

and thought I might be sick. I would have gone straight from the room if the birds hadn't all started frantically pecking at the wardrobe.

I hurried over, threw open the doors and the sight of Jem's poppet was like having an icy bucket of water thrown on top of me. There was a huge, rusty nail sticking right through its head! With a cry of dismay I grabbed the nail, dragged it free and flung it into the far corner of the room. I thought of how the ship light had come crashing down this morning, right when Jem happened to be sitting beneath it, and how his poppet had ended up with a burnt hand before, and how he kept complaining about headaches. It seemed like too big a coincidence. I'd always known that the witch hated Christian Slade but maybe her hatred for him spilled over to his descendants, too?

With a slow dawning of panic, I realized that I had made the most terrible mistake. The witch wasn't just mad, she was angry, she was dangerous and she didn't want anyone's help, least of all ours. My poppet was unharmed but it didn't make me feel any better to know it was Jem she was focusing on. I gathered up both poppets and shoved them into the little safe that had been put in the wardrobe for guests to leave their valuables. Then I slammed the door closed, keyed in a combination and hurried out of the room and down the stairs.

As I reached the bottom step I heard a low creaking of hinges and, before my eyes, the cellar door swung slowly open. I stared at it from the end of the corridor, my hand gripping tightly around the banister. I had the strongest sense that there was something crouched there, just out of sight, looking at me.

As I walked forward, there seemed to be a deep coldness beating out of that open doorway, like a long dead heart stirred back into sluggish, groaning life. My nails dug into my palms as I approached, finally stepping around the open door, face-to-face with the dark entranceway.

I'd half expected the witch to be standing there but the doorway was quite empty and the deserted staircase stretched down into grey shadows. There was a damp, mildewy smell in the cold air, stale and unpleasant. It was the smell of a place that had been shut up in the dark for too long, a place for dead things.

I strained my ears, listening for the laugh, that terrible laugh that was like spiders stroking your skin. But there was nothing except for a silence that seemed to scream and scream out of the shadows at me. In fact, a scream would almost have been better. A scream would have been easier to bear.

I knew there was something there. My eyes rested on the open doorway at the foot of the stairs, the one that led into the cellar itself. I thought it was dark and empty at first, but then I saw them.

Fingers.

There were fingers curled around the edge of the door frame. And they were bleeding. Blood clotted around the nail beds and ran in a thin line over the knuckles. It was the witch. It had to be. Suddenly, the fingers vanished and the door down there slammed, loud and hard and final, as a great rush of freezing air came racing up the staircase towards me. I stumbled back, raising my arm before my face to try to protect myself from a blow that never came. The upper door shut so hard that the entire staircase seemed to shake and a shower of dust came falling down from the ceiling, settling over my hair like a veil of spiderwebs.

A couple of waxy water beetles fell from the cracks in the wooden beams, landing with a stomach-churning splat upon the floor, their exoskeletons splitting open upon impact and a thick, viscous white goo eeking out in globs. I remembered all those water insects that had come chittering and skittering out of my hairbrush and disappeared into the floorboards upstairs. The impact of the door slamming must have shaken them loose.

But I could hardly spare a glance for the water beetles, could hardly even acknowledge them at all. Because they were nothing – nothing! – compared to the vile, awful thing that was slowly but surely dragging its massive body underneath the crack of the cellar doorway.

Chapter Thirty-One

Emma

Jem shook his head. "You can't be serious?" he said.

"I'm only telling you what happened," I replied. "My wheelchair rolled down the corridor as if there was someone pushing it. I thought the floor must be sloped but when I went along it this morning my chair never once wheeled by itself. It's just odd, that's all. This place *feels* odd. I mean, what happened to you in the library just this morning was pretty strange, wasn't it? You could have been killed."

"This building is hundreds of years old," he said, shaking his head. "Accidents like that aren't that strange. Fear breeds fear, that's all. I wish you hadn't gone to that witch museum. If Shell and I really are related to Christian Slade *and* the witch that he had put to death, then Shell's going to be even more worked up about this place."

I sighed and wrapped my hands around my mug of tea.

"God, I wish that fly would find a way out," Jem said, looking over his shoulder. "The buzzing is driving me mad. I keep hearing them around the place. I hope there isn't a dead bird in one of the chimneys."

I couldn't hear any fly and was about to say so when Jem said, "I lost my job at the Seagull yesterday."

"What do you mean you lost it? I thought they just had no more work?"

"No, I was fired."

"*Fired?* But, what—"

"Dad turned up," Jem said. "There was a scene. Word gets around. And work is finishing for the season now anyway. We've got enough money to buy food for one week, maybe two. After that, there's nothing." He rubbed his hand over his face and said, "I don't know what to do. I couldn't just leave Shell living with Dad but now I can't look after her, either. I don't want us to be split up but, winter's coming and we can't live on the street. What am I supposed to do? What would *you* do?"

I looked back at him across the table, my mind searching desperately for some magical answer.

I didn't know what he should do either.

"Honestly, Jem, I really don't think I'm qualified to dish out life advice. To anyone."

A sudden movement caught my eye and my gaze fastened on the kettle on the table between us. It was one of those old-fashioned metal ones and I could see my distorted reflection in the surface, although it was smeared with fingerprints. We'd left the door open and the doorway to the restaurant was a dark rectangle in the reflection. For a strange moment, I thought I saw something move across it, like someone running past the door.

There's no one in the restaurant, I told myself. *Concentrate on Jem or he'll think you don't give a toss about what he's trying to tell you.*

I looked back at him and saw that he was massaging his temples with his fingers.

"Headache?" I asked sympathetically.

"Yeah. Killer."

"You should take something for it."

"I have but I can't seem to shake it." He dropped his hand and looked up. "Did you hear that?"

"What?"

"It sounded like a door slamming."

Chapter Thirty-Two

Shell

It must have been twenty-five centimetres wide, as big as a dinner plate. One bright orange leg slipped out from underneath the crack in the doorway, impossibly long for any normal spider – but this was no normal spider, was it? This was a sea spider – a giant, wretched sea spider that lived in the darkest, deepest place on earth. It didn't seem to have a body, it didn't even have eyes because things that lived at the bottom of the sea didn't need eyes.

Instead it was just legs, masses of jointed legs that skittered across the floor towards me, and even though it couldn't see me it must have known I was there because its long tubular mouth was stretched out towards me eagerly...

I threw out my uninjured hand, raising it up in front of me, trying to protect myself, and the flurry of glossy wings seemed to appear out of the end of my fingertips, like magic. The black bird was there all of a sudden and, quick as a flash, it had landed on the floor in front of me, snatched up the spider, tipped back its head and swallowed the thing whole.

Pain stabbed through my nail and I looked down in time to see the tip of another bird's beak trying to force its way out from underneath. Just when I was sure it was going to rip the nail off altogether, the bird burst free and became full size, landing on the floor beside the first one in an untidy heap of feathers. A second spider came out from under the door and the second bird pounced on it instantly.

But more spiders appeared then, more than I could count, pouring out under the door, rushing towards me, intent on keeping me away from the cellar. The air filled with wings as more birds burst from the ends of my fingers, and I had never been more glad to see them in my life as they dived in, snatching spiders straight off the floor, like seagulls plucking bony fish from the freezing sea.

I staggered back, my hand found the door handle to the restaurant and I practically fell through it before slamming it closed behind me, leaning my whole body weight against it. For a few moments I could hear them out there, the flapping of wings, the snapping of beaks, the skittering of jointed legs on wooden floorboards. And then, abruptly, there was silence, and I knew, even before I opened the door, that they had gone. Like they'd never been there at all.

I opened it just a crack at first, but there was only an empty corridor in front of me. My eyes drifted to the wooden staircase, with all its carved sea creatures, and it seemed to me that there were a few more giant sea spiders there than I'd ever noticed before.

I closed the door, hurried through the restaurant and into the kitchen to join Jem and Emma.

"I made a mistake," I said, as soon as I walked in. "About the witch in the cellar."

Jem groaned. "Not this again!" He squinted at me and said, "Why is your hair all dusty?"

"We need to leave," I said. "We need to leave the Waterwitch."

"And go where?" Jem asked. "We're lucky to have somewhere to sleep at all. We can't leave just because you've worked yourself up about ghost stories and shadows."

"There is a woman here in this inn with us,"

I said, doing my very best to sound calm. "I have seen her. She exists. She wears yellow flowers in her hair, and she makes her hands bleed trying to get into Room 9, and she—"

"*What* did you say?" Jem interrupted.

The expression on his face made me feel suddenly unsure.

"I said … I said she makes her hands bleed trying to get into Room—"

"No," Jem said. "Before that."

I frowned. "She wears yellow flowers in her hair?"

For a long moment he just stared at me. Finally, he said, "Are they bird's-foot trefoil flowers?"

"Yes! So you *have* seen her!"

"Of course I haven't."

"Then how did you know about the bird's-foot trefoil?"

"They were Mum's favourite flower."

"Well, what's that got to do with—"

"You *do* remember that, don't you?" Jem pressed. He stood up and stepped towards me. "You do remember that they were Mum's favourite flower?"

"I guess."

"They came loose whenever Dad grabbed her by

her hair. And you'd get all upset and crawl around picking them up and then you'd try to give the flowers back to Mum later but she always told you to just throw them into the sea."

"Yes, I remember. But what's that got to do with the witch?"

"Oh, Shell, for God's sake, can't you see that there *is* no witch? Don't you think it's strange that she wears the exact same flowers in her hair that Mum used to? You'll be saying she has a burnt face next."

I stared at him. "But she does have a burnt face," I said. "They forced her to wear a witch's bridle and she—"

"*Mum* had a burnt face!" Jem shouted, making me jump. "Have you forgotten what happened the morning she killed herself? Is that what's been happening here – have you repressed it somehow and now it's all coming back?"

"I haven't repressed anything, and I know exactly what happened!" I replied hotly. "We were having breakfast and Dad threw a mug of scalding tea in her face. She ... she screamed and I cried and you—"

"I did nothing, just like always!" Jem practically snarled out the words. "Mum was completely alone, she had no one to help her, she— Oh, what does it matter now anyway? It happened. There's no changing it. There's no making up for it. You just ... you're not well, Shell, and you're getting things all muddled up in your mind."

I turned away from him angrily. My eyes filled with tears. And for a moment – for this one terrible, treacherous moment – I wondered whether he could possibly be right. Perhaps I *was* wrong and there was no witch haunting the inn at all. Perhaps it was just my own mind that was haunted.

"Let it hurt," Jem said quietly behind me, "and then let it go. That's the only way to get through it. You can't keep holding on to all of this, Shell, it's not good for you."

A sharp sting of pain made me look down at my hand. One of my fingers was bleeding – just a thin line of blood trickling out from my nail. I remembered the tip of a bird's beak forcing its way out and then I remembered what Kara had said to me back at her shop about a pellar's magic: *It's the kind that makes your hands bleed...*

I took a deep breath and turned back round to Jem. I wasn't wrong. I knew in my bones that the

Waterwitch was haunted, not just by Cordelia Merrick but by Christian Slade and the missing sailors as well.

"The bird's-foot trefoil *is* just a coincidence," I said. "And it's not such a strange one, either. The sea slope gets covered in that flower during the springtime, it's everywhere. I know you don't believe me but there *is* a woman here in the inn with us and she hates us but she hates you most of all. I think she's been cursing you from the moment we arrived. Maybe she was the one who sent us the keys in the first place. Maybe she wanted us to come here all along."

Jem made an impatient noise and turned away from me.

"Maybe you should think about going somewhere else," Emma said. I was so grateful I could have hugged her. "Look, whether or not the Waterwitch is really haunted, if it makes Shell feel the way that she does then it's just not a good place to be. Why don't you phone the council and register for homelessness assistance? They'll have to find somewhere for you to live then."

Jem sighed and rubbed his eyes. For a long moment he didn't speak at all. "All right," he said, at last. "Fine. I give up. I'll phone the council this afternoon."

I ran over to throw my arms around his neck and kiss him on the cheek. "Thank you," I said. "Thank you. Thank you."

"Don't thank me yet," Jem replied. "These things take time. I doubt they'll be able to find us somewhere else straight away. We might have to stay here for another couple of days."

"Then I'll call Kara and ask her to come and bless the inn."

"If it'll make you feel better, then why not? Just make it clear to her that we can't pay anything. We need all our money for food, OK? I mean it, Shell, we don't have enough to spare for an exorcism fund right now."

"It's not an exorcism, it's a blessing," I said. "Only a pellar could perform a proper exorcism."

It was all the same to Jem and I knew there was no point trying to explain the difference to him. He went upstairs to phone the council and I used my mobile to call Kara. She agreed readily enough – I think she always kind of wanted to add the Waterwitch to her collection.

She came less than an hour later. Her long black hair was tied up into a high ponytail that swished around when she moved. A few slim plaits fell amongst her loose hair, fastened at the ends with purple amethyst beads. She'd swapped her dress for jeans and a black tank top underneath a black leather jacket.

"Don't worry," she said, holding up her hand before I could say a word. "I performed an extra protection spell on myself before I came out. Whatever's down there in that cellar can scream and curse at me all it wants but it won't be able to hurt me. I promise."

"Can I do anything to help?" I asked, even though the very last thing I wanted to do was go down to that cellar.

"Nope," Kara said. "Just wait up here for me. I should only be a few minutes."

"What are you going to do?" I pressed.

"Put the witch back in the bottle, of course," Kara replied. She rummaged in her bag and drew out a glass bottle. It was a mixture of blues and greens and whites, all blended together as if many different kinds of glass had melted into each other. "It's made from sea glass," Kara said. "Perfect for a sea witch."

She handed it over to me so I could take a better look. It was a beautiful, lovely thing – far nicer than the grotty old green one that Jem and Emma had found in the fireplace all those years ago.

It rattled as I took it from her and I realized there were objects inside.

"What's in it?" I asked.

Kara counted the items off on her fingers. "Sea salt, iron nails, bird bones – don't ask me how I got those – shells, a little blood and some sand. All I have to do is say the incantation and her spirit will be drawn into the bottle."

"And what should I do with it then?"

"My suggestion? Take a boat, row out a little way and drop it into the sea. She won't be able to do any more damage there."

"Listen," I said. "Something happened here earlier."

I started to tell her about the giant sea spiders that had come swarming up from underneath the door. Kara ought to know what she was dealing with. But she hardly seemed concerned at all.

"Smoke and mirrors," she said. "They wouldn't

245

have been able to hurt you."

I felt another flare of alarm. "No, but Kara, I really think that they *could* have—"

"Shell, really, I've *got* this!" Kara said.

I could sense that I was starting to irritate her, and that's why I didn't try to say anything more and I just let her open the cellar door and walk down those steps.

Chapter Thirty-Three

Jem

I'd meant it when I told Shell we would leave the Waterwitch. I went upstairs to my room fully intending to phone the council. I found the number online, walked over to the phone by the side of the bed and picked up the receiver, but then I paused. Suddenly it didn't seem like such a good idea any more, and I couldn't remember why I had agreed to it in the first place. There was nothing wrong with the Waterwitch. Why had I let Shell persuade me into giving in to all her craziness? If I contacted the council and told them about our situation then they might split us up. This wasn't a decision I wanted to be rushing into.

I spent the next hour going over it in my mind, trying to work out what was best. Finally, I remembered what Emma had said about the Waterwitch not being a good place for Shell. I knew she was right so, once again, I picked up the phone and, this time, raised the receiver to my ear. But the dialling tone didn't sound right. It wasn't the normal electronic drone but almost more like the buzz of an insect.

I tried calling the number anyway but the buzzing didn't go away, in fact it got worse. By the time the phone was answered it was so bad that I couldn't understand the person on the other end of the line and was forced to hang up. I tried again and, this time, it didn't sound even vaguely like a dialling tone. The sound of an insect buzzing was unmistakeable. Having that noise pressed right up against my ear was unbearable and made my head throb worse than ever. I hung up and stared at the phone, wondering whether a fly could possibly have got trapped inside it.

Suddenly something landed on my arm and crawled over the skin. I was sure I'd see a fly there when I looked down, but there was nothing. I could still hear it, though — this frantic, furious buzzing that, actually, sounded more like a wasp than a fly. And it didn't seem to be coming from the phone any more but somewhere in the room instead. I frowned. Perhaps there was a nest of them. Perhaps they were in the walls. That would explain why I kept on hearing them but never saw any…

I stood up, trying to work out where the sound was coming from, but then Shell called my name from downstairs. I walked over and opened the door.

"Yes?"

"Would you come down here?"

I crossed over to the staircase and saw her standing at the bottom, staring up at me, her face pale.

"What is it?" I asked.

"It's Kara. When she went down to the cellar she said she'd only be a few minutes, but she's been there for half an hour now. I've tried calling her but she doesn't reply. Will you go and check on her? I'm too scared to go."

"All right."

I walked down the stairs and reached the bottom as Emma came in through the restaurant with Bailey.

"I'm just going to fetch Shell's friend up out of the cellar," I said before turning back to Shell. "You did tell her that we're not paying for this mumbo-jumbo, didn't you? She's not stringing this out to earn more?"

"Don't be cynical." She frowned at me. "It's not like that. Kara just wants to help."

I held up my hands. "Whatever you say."

I turned away, stepped through the open doorway, and the cold hit me like a solid wall. It was almost as if the old stones down here soaked up the chill and blasted it back out towards you. The whole place smelled musty and damp and salty somehow, like the inside of a sunken ship.

"Be careful!" Shell called out behind me.

I waved my hand at her without looking back, while silently cursing Kara for getting Shell all worked up in the first place. This was exactly the kind of thing she didn't need.

There wasn't much light on the staircase so I put my hand out against the stone to guide my way. When I got to the bottom, light from the single bulb in the cellar spilled out of the open doorway. I stepped through it and instantly saw the reason for the damp smell. The sump pump had broken and was full to the brim with dirty water that trickled over the sides and formed a large puddle on the ground around it.

There were still shelves fixed to the walls from when the room had been used as storage but, other than that, there was nothing down here except for the big fireplace where we had found the witch bottle. It had been repaired and took up almost the entire wall opposite the door.

Kara stood facing it with her back to me, muttering something. Magic words, probably. No doubt she thought she was performing some kind of spell. I'd met Kara a couple of times when Shell had dragged me into her shop and she seemed nice enough. Despite what I'd said before, Kara didn't strike me as a fraud and I thought she probably really did believe all that nonsense about broomsticks and pentacles, or whatever.

"Shell sent me down here to check on you," I said.

Kara didn't turn around. Her shoulders were moving slightly and I realized that she must be doing something with her hands.

"Do you want a cup of tea before you go?" I asked, taking a step closer. "We're about to light the stove in the library if you—"

I stopped mid-sentence.

There was blood on the floor.

Dark little droplets of it, scattered on the ground at Kara's feet.

"Kara?" I said, moving towards her.

She was still muttering something, oblivious to the fact that I was there.

I crossed the room in a few strides, walked around in front of her—

—and all the breath was sucked right out of my body.

Kara had both arms raised but it wasn't to wave her hands around in some magic-spell ritual like I'd imagined. Instead she was scratching her face, over and over and over again. The skin was peeling away and her long painted nails were gouging into angry flesh, red and raw like meat on a butcher's block. The grooves were ragged and deep, sure to leave dreadful scars that would mark her skin for the rest of her life.

In that split-second moment of horror while I stared at her, appalled, one of her acrylic nails ripped away from her finger and remained embedded in her cheek like a claw.

"Oh my God, Kara, stop!" I grabbed both her wrists and pulled them away from her face. "Stop! What the hell are you doing?"

She kept on muttering and I heard, at last, what

she was saying — the same words over and over again: "It burns, it burns, it burns, it burns, it burns, it burns…"

I felt my heart sink like a stone in my chest.

"Kara!" I shook her gently.

To my relief, she stopped muttering, her eyes focused on me and she said in a voice that was hardly more than a whisper, "Jem?"

And then she promptly burst into tears that mixed with the blood running down her face.

Chapter Thirty-Four

Shell

When Kara came up from the cellar, she looked like she'd been attacked by a deranged wild animal. Jem tried hard to persuade her to stay. He wanted to call an ambulance for her, but she was determined to leave. She wouldn't even stay at the Waterwitch long enough to wash the blood from her face. She just wanted to go home.

"But what about the witch bottle?" I said, desperate to find out. "Where is it? Did it work? Did you see the witch?"

"For God's sake, Shell, shut up about the witch!" Jem snapped.

As she refused to stay, Jem fetched his coat and said that he would walk Kara to her home above the shop, a couple of streets away. When he came back we went into the library and ate dinner around the stove in subdued silence.

"Now do you believe that there is something

wrong with the cellar?" I finally asked.

"Perhaps there's just something wrong with Kara," Jem replied. "She's obviously unstable, Shell. No sane person would do something like that. And how much do you really know about her anyway? The two of you chat in her shop but you don't hang out outside it, do you?"

"Poor Kara," Emma said with a shudder. "She seemed fine when we saw her the other day. It's hard to believe she could have had such a breakdown in such a small amount of time."

"Sometimes people just crack," Jem replied. "And you don't get any warning."

"Well, what did the council say?" Emma asked. "Are they going to find you somewhere else to live?"

"I couldn't get through," Jem said. "There's something wrong with the landline."

"Why didn't you use your mobile?" I asked.

Jem frowned. "What?"

"Your mobile. Why didn't you use your mobile?"

"I ... I don't know." He looked confused. "It didn't even occur to me."

"Do it now," I begged.

"It's too late," Jem replied. "They won't be open.

I'll do it first thing in the morning, OK?"

I pointed at him and said, "She's influencing you somehow. She stopped you from making that phone call. She's getting inside your head."

"No one is getting inside my head," Jem said irritably. "I said I'll call tomorrow – I can't do any better than that."

He rubbed at his temples with his fingertips.

"You've got a headache again, haven't you?" I asked. "You've had loads of them since you came to the Waterwitch. Don't you think that's odd?"

"Not particularly. There's been a lot going on——"

"It's because of the witch. She shoved an iron nail through a poppet I made of you. I made it for protection but she turned it into dark magic. I think she's cursing you."

"Oh, Shell, could we please not do this right now?" Jem said, dropping his hand with a sigh. "It's been a really long day and I don't even understand half of what you just said. Everyone gets headaches sometimes. It doesn't mean that you're cursed."

"What about the ship that crashed down on you this morning?" I pressed, leaning forward in my chair. "Was that just a coincidence, too? We should never have taken that witch bottle out of the fireplace. It's our fault she got out. And I think she hates Christian Slade so much that it spills over into hating us, too."

"Gran said something like that to me at the hospice," Emma said. "She said that was why she didn't want you to come back – that you were the last people who should be here."

"But didn't you find out just today that we might also be related to the woman Christian Slade accused of witchcraft?" Jem asked. "So if we're related to her, she wouldn't want to hurt us, would she?"

I thought of Dad and said, "Parents don't always love their children, though. We both know that."

Jem shook his head and looked away.

"She thinks Christian Slade had evil blood." I pressed on. "And she doesn't want there to be any more men like him."

Jem looked back at me. "Evil blood?" he said. "Well, that makes sense, at least. We come from a rotten family, Shell, and we probably do have more than our fair share of bad blood." Suddenly he leaned forward and grabbed my hand. "But we got out of there, didn't we? This is our fresh start, this is our chance to finally be normal. And the only thing standing in the way of that is the fact that you can't let go of all this witchcraft stuff."

I snatched my hand away from his. "I don't know how to make you understand," I said, feeling hurt and frustrated in equal measures. "But you're wrong this time, Jem. You're wrong. Think about it. Ever since we came here, something's been different. You don't look right. You're tired all the time, you burned your hand and now you're getting these headaches."

"She's right," Emma said. "I noticed something was off about you the day I arrived. And that day at the Seagull you—"

"Stop." Jem held up his hand and Emma fell silent. He turned back to me and said, "I've been trying to keep us safe. Do you think that's easy? It's tough, Shell, and you've only made it even harder. Of course I'm tired. Of course I feel like crap. But it's just stress. I am not cursed. And I'm not listening to this any more." He stood up. "I'm going to bed."

Chapter Thirty-Five
Shell

I went to bed soon after Jem but the image of Kara's ruined face kept replaying in my mind and I couldn't sleep. Finally, I got up, left the room and walked down the corridor past the row of closed doors. When I paused outside Room 19 I distinctly heard the sharp scratch of a match flaring to life. If I was to open the door I knew I would see a sailor leaning against the wall, looking out of the window and smoking a cigarette. I could even smell the smoke, just faintly, out in the corridor.

I hadn't been too afraid of him the first time – but then he turned to look at me and I saw that the side of his head was gone. Just gone. In its place there was a mess of blood and bone and matted hair, blobs of brain matter and jelly steadily leaking out on to his collar as he gazed at me, quite calmly, slowly exhaling smoke that swirled in the air between us. He must have been one of the sailors who'd been shot on deck by his mad crewmate. The one who saw the witch's face. *Once you see her face it's over.* That's what they said. It wasn't her face that bothered me, though, it was the laugh.

Outside Room 21 I could hear the soft creaking of a rope and knew that the dockhand who had been sent to change the *Waterwitch*'s name was in there, hanging by his neck from the rafters, slowly swinging round and round, his face purple and bloated. They were all here with us. All of them.

I briefly considered going and waking Jem up and dragging him into one of the other rooms but there was no guarantee they'd still be there by then, and there was no guarantee that he would see them even if they were smoking and bleeding and dying right in front of him.

At the staircase I paused and thought about going downstairs to Room 7 where the blood dripped from the beams and Christian Slade's tortured ghost languished in utter misery. But I'd told Emma the truth when I'd said that Christian didn't talk. He couldn't. When the beam fell on him it must have shattered part of his lower jaw. He tried to speak to me once and bits of tooth and bone and gum started falling out of his mouth.

As I stood there, thinking about it, I suddenly heard the scratch of nails on wood – a fearsome, frantic, scraping, clawing sound – and I knew that Cordelia was down there again, trying to find some way into the room. I knew that if I were to kneel down and peer through the banisters I'd see her, pressed up against the door, deepening the grooves in the wood as she dragged her nails down the door over and over and over again, until the blood ran freely down her wrists. I shuddered and turned away from the staircase.

I went back to my room and lay down in bed, staring up at the wooden beams above my head, trying to work out what I should do. I had to do something. Jem had looked after me all my life and now there was a danger here that he couldn't see and didn't believe in that I had to protect him from.

I made up my mind. First thing in the morning, I was going to see Kara. I would make her tell me how to finish the witch-bottle spell. Perhaps I could perform it even though she wasn't able to – after all, I *wanted* it a lot more than she did. I needed it. I was willing to die doing it if it meant I could save my brother. And I had the birds to help me.

I was up with the grey light of dawn, tiptoed downstairs and let myself out into the biting morning air. The cobbles were damp with tiny diamonds of sea mist and the air was cold and crisp and clear. There was a grey and gloomy feeling but I couldn't tell if it was in the air or just in my own head.

I headed towards Buller Quay where one or two of the cafes were bound to be open to serve the fishermen coming in with their catch. They were unloading crates from the boats as I walked past – lemon sole, cuttlefish and cod, brown crabs and squid. I couldn't help feeling sorry for the wide-eyed, open-mouthed fish lying in their beds of ice in their blue crates. Their open eyes were all staring and surprised and why not? They couldn't have known last night, as they swam about in their dark, peaceful, underwater world, that these were to be their last hours alive. You always thought there would be more nights, more days, more chances...

I hurried past the market and into one of the cafes

where I bought two bacon sandwiches and two coffees in paper cups with the last of my money. Then I walked around the corner to the next street where Kara's shop was. Her mum's flat was just above it and had its own separate entrance and bell. I rang it and stood waiting, hoping that Kara would answer the door instead of her mum.

In fact, Kara must already have been up and dressed – or perhaps it was just that she never got undressed last night – because she quickly came downstairs wearing the same jeans and black top from yesterday. She looked different, and not just because of her clawed face. There were no beads or plaits in her hair – it hung loose and lifeless over her shoulders. And her usual dark eye make-up was gone. Perhaps that was what made her look so washed out and pale.

In the grey morning light the deep cuts down her face looked even worse, despite the fact that she'd washed the blood away. It was hard to believe she'd really done that with her own nails. The cut beneath her right eye had gone a sort of yellowish colour and I thought it was bound to become infected.

I held up the paper bag. "I brought you some

breakfast," I said quietly.

Kara looked from me to the bag for a moment, then she sighed and said, "Let me fetch my jacket."

We walked around to Banjo Pier. They'd put a sign out to say it was closed, meaning they must be expecting bad weather, but we just stepped over it and made our way down the stone walkway. They closed the pier in bad weather because there were no railings to hold on to if a high wave tried to drag you away but locals knew when it was safe to go down there and when it wasn't.

Kara and I sat on the curved seat that ran around the circular section right at the end of the pier. From there we could watch the trawlers, netters and mackerel boats returning to the harbour. I opened the bag and handed Kara the bacon sandwich and coffee and, for a few minutes, we sat eating in silence.

The bacon sandwich was greasy and the coffee was cold and tasted like the plastic cup it was contained in. Kara didn't seem too impressed, either, or perhaps she just wasn't hungry, because she started ripping off pieces of the sandwich and throwing it out to the seagulls who flapped and shrieked and pecked at each other as they fought to get to the scraps first.

I wondered if seagulls should really be eating bacon – wasn't it kind of unnatural for them to be eating pig? – but I didn't say anything.

"I was here on the pier one time and someone was feeding the seagulls and then this fat pigeon wandered in out of nowhere," Kara said. "And the seagulls killed it." She didn't look at me, but stared out at the returning fishing boats instead. As the waves battered against the side of the pier, sea spray blew into our faces and I was sure the salt must be stinging her cuts like anything but she didn't flinch or turn her face away. "They tore it apart right in front of us," she went on. "There was blood and feathers smeared all around the place." She glanced at me. "That's why they tell you not to feed them, isn't it? It makes them go a bit mad. It was high tide, too, the fishing boats were coming back and there was blood in the water. Perhaps that made it worse, perhaps they could smell it and that's why they went berserk like that."

"Kara, what happened in the cellar?" I asked, tossing the remains of my sandwich in the bin. I hadn't come here to talk about seagulls. My hair was wet with spray now and sticky with salt on the back of my neck. "Why didn't it work? What went wrong?"

"I couldn't say the incantation," Kara said. "It was like there were spikes pressing into my tongue, preventing me."

She put a hand to her mouth and lapsed into silence.

Spikes pressing into her tongue. Of course. The witch's bridle.

I took a piece of paper and a pen from my pocket and handed them over to her. "Could you write the incantation down for me?"

Kara took them from me reluctantly and scribbled down the words before passing the pen and paper back. "It won't do you any good," she said quietly. "Don't go down to the cellar, Shell. Leave the Waterwitch as soon as you can and don't ever think of the place again."

Suddenly, I caught a snatch of the witch's laughter, faint at first – you could almost mistake it for the wind – but I could hear it clear as anything, shrieking over the thundering waves slamming relentlessly into the pier and spraying us with salt. The weather was getting worse. Maybe we shouldn't be here after all.

"Can you hear that laugh?" I asked. Kara was

a witch, too, so there was no reason to think she wouldn't be able to hear Cordelia now, not when the laugh was shrill and loud enough to slice through the top of your head.

I glanced at Kara only to find her staring back at me with the strangest expression on her face.

"Shell," she said, "*you're* the one who's laughing."

I stared back at her, incredulous, remembering how Emma had said the exact same thing to me back at the Waterwitch.

"Don't *say* that!" I glared at her. "It's not *me* laughing, it's *her*! There it was again! You must have heard it that time, you *must* have!"

Kara stood up. The wind had picked up and plucked the sandwich wrapper from her hands, carrying it over the side to the water below. The gulls must have thought it was food because they went screaming after it in a frenzy of feathers. "I heard *you* laugh," Kara said. "And no one else."

I stood up, too.

To my surprise, Kara took a step backwards, and her legs bumped up against the stone wall.

That laugh came again, carried in on the south-westerly gale that drove the trawlers racing back into the shelter and safety of the harbour. The sound crawled over my skin and I shuddered from head to toe. Kara went even paler than before and I didn't blame her. There was no amusement in that sound – only madness. It was all twisted up and wrong, like seagulls eating pigs, and boats trapped inside bottles, and dads that broke your bones and weren't sorry afterwards, weren't sorry at all. It was like looking at the world from the other side of a mirror and finding everything was upside down and the wrong way round.

"You're already cursed," Kara said, staring at me. "There's nothing you can do. Leaving the Waterwich won't help. The witch's curse will follow you to the ends of the earth. Once you're cursed there's no hope."

The wind made tangled birds' nests of our hair as it whipped around our faces, and I think I knew what Kara was going to do even before she did. Her eyes slid away from me and out towards the sea – perhaps she heard the witch laughing out on the water after all – and then the monstrous grey wave was rolling towards us, rising up out of the ocean like a hand with outstretched fingers.

Too late, I remembered the sailor on the *Waterwitch* all those years ago. I saw Kara turn towards the wall, and I reached my hand out towards her and my fingers even came into contact with the butter-soft leather of her jacket but I was too late to stop her. In one movement she was over the side and the wave closed around her like a fist, leaving my hand grasping at air.

I ran to the side of the wall and leaned over as far as I dared. For a moment, I thought I saw Kara's dark hair in the water and I grabbed the life-saving ring hanging from the rails, but when I turned back I saw that it wasn't hair floating there at all, but seaweed.

"Kara!" I screamed into the wind. "Kara!"

She never answered. The waves crashed into the pier over and over again, covering everything with foam and flecks of sand and shattered shells, and although my eyes darted around everywhere, I just couldn't see her, I just couldn't see her. In the end I was forced to throw the ring out at random before running back down the pier to fetch help. I knew, deep down, that it was too late. But sometimes you just have to scream for help anyway, even when you know that there is absolutely nothing anyone can do to help you.

Chapter Thirty-Six

Shell

The coastguard sent out a search party for Kara and wanted me to wait, but I couldn't stay. I knew in my bones that Kara was gone, and if they found her then it would already be too late. I had to get back to the Waterwitch and get that witch bottle before I lost my nerve.

As I hurried back through the cobbled streets I tried not to think about what had just happened but I kept seeing Kara inside my head, drowned at the bottom of the ocean, swallowed up by a monster that was always hungry no matter how many shipwrecks and souls it gobbled up. I felt a sob rise in my chest and had to push it back down hard. There was no time for falling apart now.

As I got closer to the inn, I heard angry voices – voices that I recognized – and all thoughts of Kara went out of my mind. I felt almost like a sleepwalker as I turned into the street and saw Jem and Dad.

The last time I saw Dad was the day of my accident, and it felt odd seeing him now. Part of me wanted to run to him but the other part wanted to run *from* him, and the two conflicting urges seemed like they might tear me right down the middle, like I was a paper doll. That's what it feels like to love someone you're afraid of, I guess – just the worst feeling in the whole entire world.

"You're responsible!" Dad was yelling at Jem. "If you hadn't taken my keys then I wouldn't have missed the boat. Now I have no goddamn job and it's your fault!"

Jem tried to say something but it was no good trying to talk to Dad when he was angry. He went to a place where he couldn't hear you, where he couldn't hear anything beyond the small, angry thing screaming and shouting inside his own head. When I was little I used to imagine the angry man in Dad's head as one of those circus strongmen, with muscles bulging everywhere and a very large moustache and very small eyes. Horrible to look at but cartoonish and buffoonish – nothing really, truly frightening. I knew better than that now. There was no circus strongman inside Dad's head, there was a devil instead. A devil that hated us and wanted Dad to hate us, too.

The shouting must have been audible from inside the Waterwitch because the door opened and Emma came out, her hand on Bailey's collar. She stopped dead when she saw Dad — she knew enough about our family to realize it was a very bad thing that he had turned up here like this. I didn't know whether Dad had found out somehow that we were staying at the Waterwitch or if he'd just been hanging around outside the Seagull but, either way, he was here now, and the thought flashed through my mind that it was the curse, that this was how the witch was going to hurt us.

For a moment, the puddles on the cobbles looked like blood, dark and gleaming. I blinked hard and, when I opened my eyes, they were just water again, still and flat as a mirror, reflecting the Waterwitch back at me, with pale faces in the windows and black birds on the roof.

"I'm not giving you any more money," Jem said coldly. "What happened to the taxi fare I gave you that night? I suppose you drank it?"

The truth always made Dad the maddest of all. We learned that a long time ago. So I could tell that

272

what Jem had said was true by the way Dad reacted. I'd seen him fly off the handle before, many times, but it never got any easier to watch.

He reached into his pocket and, suddenly, there was a boning knife in his hand and I felt this sick feeling of dread, a feeling I knew well.

"You ungrateful little shit," he said, glaring at Jem and speaking in a harsh, ugly whisper.

"Dad!" I called out. I had no idea what I was going to say – my only thought was to distract him. He couldn't be looking at my brother like that – not when he had a knife in his hand. Suddenly I was back in the car with the melted ice cream all those years ago, trembling and letting Jem take the beating and the blame for something I had done. I couldn't let that happen again. This time I had to make some kind of difference. Behind me, more birds gathered on the roof of the Waterwitch. I could hear their wings rustling. They were up there, watching and waiting – waiting for the thing they'd been watching and waiting for their entire lives.

Dad turned at my voice and almost seemed to recoil from me, taking a step back on the cobbles. "You stay right where you are!" he said, pointing the knife at me. "Take one step closer and I swear to God you'll regret it!"

"If you don't leave in the next five seconds, I'm calling the police," Emma said, and I winced to hear her talk to Dad like that because I knew he would never accept that kind of tone from anyone.

Sure enough, the next moment he was striding towards her, the knife still gripped in his hand, his knuckles completely white.

And I guess Bailey thought that Emma was in danger and that he had to protect her because he charged forwards, his collar ripped right out of Emma's hand, and he was barking and snarling at Dad in the street, his hackles raised, his upper lip drawn back and his teeth gleaming pale and sharp, like a wolf in the grey morning light.

Emma lunged up out of her chair to try to grab him but she was too late to stop what happened next. The knife in Dad's hand flashed once, and then it was coming down and coming down and coming down.

There was an awful sound – somewhere between a yelp and a howl – and then Bailey was lying on the cobbles and there was blood on his fur, slick and metallic. Emma's cry of anguish went right through me as she dropped down on the floor beside her dog. Jem was running towards Dad and suddenly I could see what was going to happen – I could see it clear as day, as if I was staring straight into a witch ball.

Dad would spin around to meet Jem and then the boning knife would bury itself in my brother's neck and nothing would ever be OK again. I ran forwards without thinking about what I was doing, and the birds came off the roof behind me, claws scraping against slate as they spread their black wings against the salt-coloured sky.

"*No!*" I snarled the word, reaching Dad first, before Jem, and shoving him square in the chest with my free hand.

Dad turned his head to look down at me and, for just a moment, the angry mask that made him look like an ape was replaced with a look of childlike fear. Then the wall of birds hit him in a flurry of feathers and wings and beaks and claws.

Dad staggered back into the street, both hands clutching at his chest, a gasp of pain bubbling up out of his throat. The birds wriggled underneath his fingers, squirmed their way beneath his shirt and then dug their beaks deeper and deeper into his chest, pulling out lumps of flesh and strands of hair.

Dad went down on his knees, then curled up sideways on the cobbles, jerking and twitching. I knew the birds were tearing out his heart in chunks and I was glad. I was *glad*! I wanted him to die. I loved him but I wanted him gone because loving someone so cruel was too hard and would never get any easier.

Somebody called an ambulance and the birds left when the paramedics arrived. Nobody saw them go except for me. Nobody knew what had *really* just happened. The ambulance crew said that Dad had had a massive heart attack, and pronounced him dead at the scene. Natural causes, they said.

But I couldn't think of a more unnatural way to die.

Chapter Thirty-Seven

Emma

I couldn't feel the pain in my back because the pain in my heart obliterated everything else. My arms were around Bailey, my hands on his coat were sticky with blood. He whined softly and tried to lick my face. The knife had got his shoulder and I tried to tell myself that a shoulder wasn't too bad, that at least it hadn't been his chest or head, that perhaps he would be OK.

Someone said they would drive us to the nearest vet. I didn't want to let go of him. I wanted to pick him up and carry him myself but, of course, I couldn't.

"I'll take him," Jem said, there at my side. "Give him to me, Em."

"Be careful!" I said as Jem lifted him up in his arms.

Someone else helped me to stand up and, in the first moments after my spine uncurled, the pain was so sickeningly bad that I really thought I might pass out. But I couldn't let Bailey down, I couldn't not be with him.

When someone started fussing about my wheelchair I practically screamed at them to leave it there. All that mattered was getting to the vet's as quickly as possible. Soon, Jem, Shell and I were in the back seat of someone's car, with Bailey on our laps.

From the window I could see the paramedics lifting Jem and Shell's father on to a gurney and I could almost believe that he was still alive, that he wasn't really dead at all. I expected him to sit up at any moment and call after us but, instead, his body remained limp and lifeless, one hand hanging over the edge of the gurney. I'd never seen a dead body before and my mind reeled with the fact that I was seeing one now. Jem and Shell were staring out the window at him, too, and it was as if our eyes were locked on the sight. The ambulance's blue lights flashed over everything, making it all look like a scene from a film. It was a relief when the car pulled around the corner and the sight was left behind, breaking the spell.

Bailey whined and I talked to him softly, telling him he would be OK. He kept licking my hands, but he seemed suddenly older to me than he ever had before and there seemed to be too many grey hairs on his muzzle. This was my fault, all my fault.

Finally, we were at the vet's and Bailey was rushed off. My walking stick was back with my wheelchair so Jem practically had to carry me to my seat in the waiting room. I didn't think I'd ever felt so helpless before in my whole life.

Chapter Thirty-Eight
Shell

"Jem? Can I speak to you alone for a minute?"

I knew he didn't want to leave Emma but he followed me into the cold air outside.

"Why did he have to bring a knife with him, for God's sake?" he said. He kicked a bin nearby and the metal clanged too loudly in the cold air. "He always was his own worst enemy. It's no wonder he had a heart attack with all that rage he carried around all the time."

I clenched my hands into fists. Jem was wrong; it wasn't Dad's rage that had killed him – it was mine. I saw the birds swoop down on him once again in a flurry of black wings; bloody beaks ripping out chunks of flesh, frantic to get to his heart. I couldn't talk about Dad right now, not even to Jem. I couldn't think about what I had just done. I couldn't look down at my own hands in case I saw blood dripping from them.

"I have to tell you about something that happened earlier," I said. "I think Kara is dead."

"*What?*" Jem stared at me.

"I went to see her this morning. We had breakfast at Banjo Pier. And, right at the end, she ... she jumped into the water."

"Oh my God! Why? What happened?"

The witch cursed her, I wanted to say, but that would only lead to an argument so I just shook my head and said, "I don't know. I guess she was still upset about yesterday. The coastguard went out to try to find her but ... I think it will be too late."

"You don't know that," Jem said at once. "Perhaps they've already found her. Perhaps she's fine." He glanced back towards the vet's and said, "Let's not jump to any conclusions until we find out what's actually happened."

Chapter Thirty-Nine

Jem

The vet came out into the waiting room just as Shell and I walked back in.

"It looks worse than it is," she said. "The knife got his shoulder but didn't hit any arteries. The shock isn't ideal for a dog of his age but we've cleaned the wound and stitched it up and I think he'll be OK. We've given him painkillers and he's sleeping now. We'll keep an eye on him here overnight but, all being well, you can take him home in a day or two."

We got a taxi back to Looe. Emma's wheelchair was still there where we had left it on the street so I helped her into it and then the three of us went back into the Waterwitch, straight to our rooms to change our blood-stained clothes. I found Emma in the library afterwards and sat down in the armchair opposite her. "I'm so sorry, Em," I said.

She looked at me. "For what?"

"For everything. For Bailey most of all."

"It's not your fault," she replied.

"It's not yours, either." I reached out for her hand.

"He's my responsibility," she said. "Of course it's my fault. I should have kept him safe."

I wanted to tell her that she shouldn't feel guilty, that there was nothing she could have done but the guilt would be there whatever I said so the words would have been meaningless and empty, hollow and useless. Worse than saying nothing at all.

"I know what it feels like," I said instead.

Emma gave me a bleak look. "You know what it feels like to have a disability assistance dog who is faithful and loyal and—" She bit her lip and I could tell she was trying not to cry. "And changes your world and saves your life and is your best friend for six years and then gets stabbed trying to defend you?"

"No. But I know what it's like when someone you love gets hurt and you feel like you didn't do enough to stop it," I said.

Emma put her head in her hands and said through her fingers, "I'm sorry. At least you were able to make a difference to Shell, though. You took her away."

I shook my head. "My biggest fear for Shell was never Dad. It was the demons in her own head. Mum had them and Shell has them, too. When Mum killed herself and Shell found her, it got worse. This thing with the birds. And now, today, she saw Dad die right in front of her…" I frowned, hearing myself say the words, feeling them sink into my brain. "I'd better go and check on her. Make sure she's OK."

Chapter Forty

Shell

When I came face-to-face with the cellar door, I wanted to be brave and strong, but I felt nothing but fear.

My birds gathered around my feet, staring at the door before us. I remembered how they had protected me from those hideous sea spiders, how they'd flown at Dad, and I understood, at last, what the birds were, what they had always been. They weren't familiars at all – they were the magic itself. Pure magic that happened to have shining eyes and glossy wings and had been desperate to get out of me all along, get out and fly like they were supposed to.

I reached my trembling hand out slowly towards the door. When it was almost there I dropped it and shook my head.

"I can't," I whispered. "I can't, I can't, I just can't."

I hated that I was such a terrible coward but I

turned away from the birds and walked into the library where I found Emma alone by the fire. Jem would be back soon and I knew I didn't have much time. I had to talk to her quickly, before he came back. He was far more likely to listen to her.

"Jem's looking for you," Emma said, as soon as I walked in. "He wanted to make sure that you're—"

"Emma, please," I cut her off. I wanted to sound calm and in control, but my voice shook as I spoke. "Please speak to Jem. Tell him that we've got to leave, that we can't stay in this place another minute. He'll listen to you – I know he will. I can't stay here any more, I really can't. I'd rather sleep on the streets! I'd rather be anywhere other than here! I'd almost rather be dead!"

I started to cry; I couldn't help it. It was all just too much.

A hand took hold of my arm and I realized that Jem had come into the room behind me, that he'd heard every word I'd said. I was afraid he'd be angry, that he'd get frustrated with me again, that he'd tell me to pull myself together. But instead he put his arms around me and held on to me tight.

"We'll leave," he said quietly. "We'll leave today."

Chapter Forty-One
Shell

The Seagull still had rooms free so Emma booked us in for the night. She took a room on the ground floor and Jem and I took the twin room next door. We didn't even stop to pack more than a change of clothes – Jem said he would go back for our stuff later. I took the poppets from the wardrobe and, when we got to the Seagull, put them straight in the safe. But Kara's words kept trying to sneak back into my brain and spoil my sense of relief: *The witch's curse will follow you to the ends of the earth… Once you're cursed there's no hope…*

I blocked them out, refused to listen to them. Maybe we would be OK now that we had left the Waterwitch. Maybe it was over. Even Dad couldn't hurt us any more. We were safe.

Jem tried to talk to me about Dad once we got to the Seagull, wanting to know how I felt about what had happened, but the truth was that I didn't feel anything. Just nothing. Just numb. It didn't seem real. Part of me couldn't help thinking that he wasn't really dead at all; he was back at his cottage, getting into his overalls, preparing to go out on the fishing boats.

When we went downstairs, everyone at the Seagull was talking about the girl who had jumped off the end of the pier that morning and we heard that her dead body had been found a couple of hours later by the coastguard. I tried to feel something – some sadness or regret or guilt – but I only had the same numb feeling I had about Dad.

I wasn't surprised when Jem took me aside and said, "I think you need to go to the police station. If you don't speak to them then they might think you had something to do with what happened to Kara. If they ask for your address, tell them that we're staying at the Seagull at the moment and that we're going to register with the council for homelessness assistance today."

"Maybe we can go back to the cottage?" I said hopefully. "Now that Dad's gone?"

"Maybe," Jem said, although he sounded doubtful. "But Dad changed the locks, remember?

I don't know what's going to happen next, Shell. I don't know how this is going to work. We'll just have to wait and see."

I didn't care about what happened next. The only thing that mattered was that we were out of the Waterwitch. We left Emma at the Seagull and Jem and I went to the police station and I gave my statement. Jem told them that I would have been in before but that our father had died unexpectedly that morning. It felt weird hearing him say that and, for a minute, I didn't believe him. It still didn't feel like something that had actually happened. When I tried to think about it – about what the birds had done to him – my mind just slid away from it.

By the time we'd finished at the police station, the council offices were closed, so Jem said we would have to go and see them about housing the next day. We returned to the Seagull and had dinner in the restaurant with Emma. It felt wrong seeing her without Bailey and I was sure she must miss him unbearably.

After dinner we sat quietly together in the lounge for a little while but, even though it was still fairly early, Jem was practically falling asleep in his chair.

"Why don't you go to bed?" Emma finally said. "You look like you're about to keel over."

She was right and I felt a cold niggle of worry. But Jem would sleep better now that we weren't in the Waterwitch, I was sure of it. We all would.

"I think I will, actually," Jem said. He tried to smile and said, "Long day."

"I'll go with you," I said, standing up.

We said goodnight to Emma, agreed to meet for breakfast the next morning, and returned to our room.

"It's weird, isn't it?" I said as I walked in.

"What is?"

"Dad being gone."

Jem paused. "Yes," he said, closing the door. "It is weird."

I remembered how he had tried to ask me how I felt about it earlier but it hadn't occurred to me to ask him back. I did so now.

"I don't know," Jem replied. He looked at me and said, "It's complicated, isn't it?"

I nodded. It was always complicated with Dad. Always.

Jem sighed. "I just wish he could have been less

difficult. I wish that it hadn't ended … like that."

I felt a painful flash of guilt. It was my fault. It was my birds who'd killed him.

"Maybe I shouldn't have taken his keys that night after all," Jem muttered. He shook his head and said, "I don't know. I'm going to bed."

I went into the bathroom to brush my teeth. By the time I came out, Jem was already asleep. I crawled into the other bed and switched off the lamp.

I woke up just a few hours later and, for a moment, I wasn't sure where I was. The shadowy room seemed unfamiliar in the dark so I switched on the light, and remembered we were in the Seagull. We were safe.

And then I heard the buzzing. The frantic droning buzz of an enraged insect. I gazed around in confusion, and quickly saw it: there was a water wasp on Jem's pillow, wriggling around on its back, trying to right itself. Suddenly, it managed to flip over and then, to my absolute horror, it scuttled straight up the side of Jem's face and disappeared, wriggling and squirming, into his ear.

"No!" I cried, throwing back the covers. My bare feet landed on the floor with a horrible soft crunch. I looked down and saw that the floor was swarming with water wasps, their large red eyes gleaming like blood in the lamplight. Their brown bodies squelched and their red eyes popped beneath my feet; they crawled up my ankles, biting and stinging, but I didn't care as I ran towards Jem's bed.

My birds flapped into the air to help, gobbling up the wasps on the floor, pecking them from my feet, but there were so many of the insects and they weren't slow and lumbering like the spiders, they were lightning fast. I couldn't get to Jem's bed quickly enough. The wasps were heading straight for him and – even as I screamed out his name – I saw three, four, five more of the terrible, awful things crawl into his ear and disappear.

I snatched my hairbrush up from the bedside table just as he opened his eyes, and brought it down as hard as I could on the pillow, crushing one of the wasps.

Jem jerked back, instantly wide awake. I raised the hairbrush to swat another wasp that was wriggling its way up the duvet but Jem tore the brush from my hand and threw it into the corner of the room.

"What the hell are you doing?" he gasped. "Have you completely lost your mind?"

"There were wasps!" I said. "Water wasps everywhere!"

But when I gazed around, they had gone, and so had the birds. The room looked completely ordinary. There wasn't even a squashed wasp on the pillow.

"Some of them crawled right into your ear—" I started to say.

"For God's sake, Shell, you were dreaming again," Jem snapped. "Please, just go back to bed."

He yanked the quilt back up to his neck and then rolled over, facing the wall with his back to me. I looked down at my feet, expecting to see angry red sting marks where the skin still throbbed, but there was nothing there.

I crossed the room and drew back the curtains, intending to look out at the Waterwitch. Only I couldn't because something was covering the window, and I couldn't work out what it was at first. Then I saw that the glass was crawling with hundreds of water wasps. Their horrid brown undersides were pressed up against the glass, exposing the thorax and abdomen, their six hairy legs flailing all over the place as they sought for purchase on the slippery surface.

Then they dropped away from the window all together at the same moment, swarming away across the street, heading directly for the Waterwitch. A single solitary light shone from one of the windows, turning the figure there into a dark, still silhouette. All I could make out was the long hair over her shoulders as she stood motionless, staring across the street at us. The water wasps went straight to the same window, squirming in through the little cracks in the brickwork and the small spaces around the windowpane.

Slowly, she raised her hand and smeared blood across the window with her bleeding fingertip until one word stared back at me, thin trails running down from the red letters:

Exodus 34:7.

Then the light went out and the woman was lost from my view, but I could still feel her over there – could feel the burn of her stare, prickling over my skin even after I yanked the curtains closed and stumbled back a few steps.

I knew about the Book of Exodus from the Bible because it was the one that the witch hunters had relied on all those years ago, the one with that hateful, poisonous verse: *Thou shalt not suffer a witch to live.*

I took out the Bible left in the top drawer by the side of the bed but it was a New Testament. The Book of Exodus was in the Old Testament, so I picked up my phone and Googled it. The first page of search results came back with one phrase that repeated over and over again: *generational curse.*

Fear crept down my back as I clicked on the first result and read the verse for Exodus 34:7:

"Keeping mercy for thousands, forgiving iniquity and transgression and sin, but that will by no means clear the guilty. Punishing the iniquity of the fathers upon the children, and upon the children's children, unto the third and the fourth generation."

Kara's words played over and over again inside my head as I switched off the phone: *The witch's curse will follow you to the ends of the earth...*

Once you're cursed there's no hope. No hope at all...

When I woke up the next morning, I knew instantly that something was wrong. Jem's bed was empty but I could hear him in the bathroom, and it sounded like he was being sick. I sat up in bed and instantly saw the birds, all gathered on the floor around the wardrobe. But they weren't pecking at it frantically like last time. Instead they were just staring up at it in silence, and that made me feel more afraid somehow. It was as if they knew there was no point in freaking out and trying to get my attention because something bad had already happened and it was too late to do anything about it...

I walked over, opened the door and punched in the combination code to the safe. Then I heard myself make this awful moan at the sight of the poppets. In my head I could hear Jem asking me again about the missing nails from the cellar door:

Did you pick those nails up off the floor? I can't find them...

Well, now, here they all were. There must have been twenty nails stuck into the poppet I had made of Jem. They'd been driven through the head, the arms, the stomach, the face, everywhere. I felt my eyes fill with tears as I grabbed one of the nails and tried to tug it free but it wouldn't budge. When I kept pulling, the fabric of the doll started to tear, but no dried herbs or lavender spilled out like I had expected. At first I thought the cold things falling through my fingers were pins and needles but then I realized what they actually were: coffin nails – only ever used in the darkest spells of malice. You didn't use them if you just wanted to hurt someone.

You used them when you wanted them dead and decaying in their graves.

Chapter Forty-Two
Emma

I knew it would take me longer than usual to get ready in the morning without Bailey's help so I set my alarm early. When I was finally dressed I went next door to meet the others. But when I knocked on the door, Shell answered and I could tell instantly something was wrong.

"What's up?" I asked.

"It's Jem," she almost whispered. "He's not well."

He came out of the bathroom just then and I was startled to see that his eyes were bloodshot and his T-shirt was actually stuck to him with sweat.

"I think I've got the flu," he announced, staggering over to the bed.

Shell hurried over to him and when her hand brushed against his skin she gasped. "You're burning up!"

"That's what happens when you get flu," Jem said, pushing her hand away. "Don't touch me. You don't want to catch it."

"Is there anything we can do?" I asked.

"No, I think … I think I'm just going to lie here," Jem said, crawling back beneath the covers. We left him shivering in his bed and went downstairs to the breakfast room.

"He's just got flu," I said gently to Shell, seeing how distressed she looked.

"He's been ill-wished," she replied. "It's the wasps. The water wasps in his head."

"*Wasps?*" I stared at her. "What wasps?"

"I saw them crawl inside his ear last night. The witch sent them. And she attacked his poppet. It's the curse."

"Shell, look—"

"I have to go back to the Waterwitch," she said. "I have to face the witch. It's the only way."

"If you want to go back then I'll go with you," I said. "Why don't we have some breakfast and then the vet's will be open and I can call for an update about Bailey. After that we'll go across together. OK?"

Shell shrugged but I decided to take that as a yes. She didn't want any breakfast so I ate by myself and then left her in the lounge while I went back to my room to call the vet. The receptionist answered the call and then put me on hold while she went to find the right person. As I sat there waiting, my heart sank as I looked through the window and saw Shell go across the street, straight to the Waterwitch. She must have taken the keys from Jem's bag because she disappeared inside, closing the door behind her.

I sighed. She'd be all right over there by herself for a minute. I'd just have to catch her up once I got off the phone.

Chapter Forty-Three

Shell

When I walked into the Waterwitch, I took Jem's poppet from my pocket and tried once again to pull out those dreadful nails but they were driven in so deeply that I was afraid forcing them out would rip the entire doll to shreds. Perhaps that was what the witch wanted me to do. I shoved the poppet back in my pocket and reached out for the cellar door instead.

This time, I gripped the handle firmly and pulled the door open, exposing the bare stone staircase that led down into the dark. Inexplicably, there was a glass witch ball right behind the door – one of the blue ones – and my movement caused it to roll forwards, falling from step to step with a crash, like a strange and beautiful slinky, all the way to the bottom where it rolled smoothly and silently into the cellar.

I stepped on to the staircase after it and the birds followed me, flowing down the steps like a dark river.

With every footstep, I expected to see her appear there in the doorway, the witch's bridle spitting blood and red-hot ash. But it remained quite empty, although the chill in the air deepened with every step. And this was no ordinary chill – it wasn't the chill of cellars and inns but the darker, colder chill of the sea and the shipwrecks rotting at the bottom of it. How did the old rhyme go?

From Pentire Point to harbour light, a watery grave by day or night.

There were six thousand wrecks off the Cornish coast. The gales could be ferocious and the water could be treacherous even without smugglers deliberately shining false lights to wreck boats on the rocks. And here we had our very own shipwreck on dry land and it seemed wrong all of a sudden, disrespectful somehow, to have salvaged the wood from the seabed like that, almost like plucking bones from a grave.

By the time I reached the doorway at the foot of the stairs, the coldness had intensified unbearably. The room was full of witch balls. They glinted their jewel colours back at me out of the darkness, scattered about in random piles. This must have been where they went at night, drawn to Cordelia like iron filings drawn to a magnet. Beyond the balls I could see the witch bottle, lying on the floor in the far corner of the room. It didn't seem to be broken.

I kept my eyes fixed on it as I stepped forward. If Cordelia was here then the trick was not to look at her, not to see her face.

But even though my eyes were fixed on the bottle and I was deliberately not looking around the room, I knew that she was in there with me, over in the opposite corner, staring and staring and just daring me to look back. The birds must have understood the danger because they rose up together in a kind of protective wall all around me, shielding me from the witch with their wings so that I couldn't give in to the temptation to look at her.

My trembling fingers closed around the cold neck of the bottle and I snatched it up before turning on my heel and sprinting back across the room and up the stairs two at a time, dark wings flapping around me all the while. I kept expecting to feel a cold hand suddenly grip my ankle and yank me back down – I could almost see Cordelia dragging herself up the steps behind me, blood dripping out from underneath her mask – and it took all my willpower not to look.

But then I was on the last step, and I was tumbling out into the corridor, and I was out of there and I had done it, I had really done it!

The relief and triumph that surged through me lasted only an instant, though, before I heard her laughter above me. She was right there on the monster staircase. I knew that I absolutely *must not* look at her, but, somehow, my eyes found her face in the shadows with an awful inevitability.

The witch's bridle was still fastened around Cordelia Merrick's face and the smell of burning flesh and hair filled the air and filled my mouth and filled my head. Her green eyes glittered out of the dark at me but they were the only human thing left about her. The skin around the metal muzzle was a mixture of livid red and burnt black. Her eyelids had drooped and her eyes didn't seem to fit properly in their sockets any more. The lower part had sunken in, fallen away to expose a pink jelly-like substance between her eyeballs and the inflamed skin of her cheeks.

For the longest time I thought I was screaming but, in fact, there was no sound coming out of my mouth. A patchwork of bloodstains marked the front of her dress – from fresh scarlet to old brown. Her hands hanging at her sides were marked, too, her fingers red, the nails torn away from where she had been clawing and tearing at the door of Room 9.

As I stared, wanting to scream but too afraid even to do that, Cordelia tried to speak but all that came out was a pained gurgle, followed by a fresh trickle of red dribbling out from the small, square mouth hole. I could almost feel the prongs cutting up her cheeks, and the spikes impaling her tongue, and I wondered how much of it was left after all these years. It must be sliced to ribbons by now.

Cordelia tried once more to speak but no words came out of her ruined mouth, only blood and saliva, chunks of gum and chips of broken tooth. Then she tipped her head back and laughed and laughed. A couple of bird's-foot trefoil fell from her hair as she melted back into the shadows, the yellow petals scattering on the steps, so pretty there in the dark.

A red mist seemed to fill my vision and I rubbed my eyes, wondering if I had blood in them. All of a sudden the witch bottle didn't seem so important any more. All that mattered was never, ever, ever hearing that laugh again.

"Make it stop," I whispered to the birds that were suddenly lined up along the stairs, peering at me through the banisters.

I tried to tell myself that I must not let the witch's madness creep into my brain, I must not let my thoughts turn to suicide and death. I didn't want to die, I didn't. I mustn't let her trick me into thinking that I did. But then the laugh started up again and I clamped my hands over my ears and groaned aloud. I couldn't bear hearing that sound any more. It was an agony, like something that was trying to hollow me out from the inside – like that boning knife Dad had been brandishing around yesterday. I'd seen him using it on fresh catch before down at the docks, pulling out those fish spines in a single sweeping movement that only came with years and years of practice.

I would never see Dad pull out fish spines ever again.

Because he was dead.

And I had killed him.

I had killed him.

This weird sob burst out of me and I didn't know why I was crying. I had wanted him to die, after all, the birds had only done what I had told them to do.

But, suddenly, there was this great, gaping, black hole, like a cannon had passed through my chest. Dad was actually dead. He was really gone.

Gone, and gone, and gone. Because of me.

There were hundreds of birds now, bunched up together on the wooden staircase of carved sea monsters. They were all staring at me with their sad, shining black eyes, like polished beads in their heads, and I could tell that they pitied me. I pitied myself. What a mess I had made of things. I couldn't even manage to save myself, let alone Jem.

I turned away from the reproachful black gaze of my magical birds, and walked into the restaurant. For a flash of a second, I saw all the crew of the *Waterwitch* sitting at the empty tables, but they weren't eating and I supposed it was because of the rats, swarming all over the place, fleeing the sinking ship as it went down into the depths.

Then I blinked and they were gone. I hurried across the room, walking straight to the jar of fish hooks on the mantelpiece. They were freezing cold against my skin, as if they'd been deep-chilled at the bottom of the sea, and the tiny barbs on the end looked monstrously cruel.

I reached into the jar, grabbed the biggest hook and was just about to pull it out when a movement caught my eye and I looked up at the massive oil painting that hung there.

It had changed. The *Waterwitch* was no longer sailing on a stormy sea – instead it was a wreck resting on the seabed. Ships had souls. Someone had told me that once – perhaps it was Dad. All ships had souls, he said. Maybe that was why there was something so profoundly melancholy about the sight of a sunken ship, decaying at the bottom of the ocean, abandoned and alone.

Clutching the hook, I staggered back from the painting a couple of steps, smashing the jar in the process and slicing one of my fingers, scattering fish hooks and pieces of glass everywhere. I couldn't take my eyes off the painting. The hundreds of barnacles clinging to its prow made the ship look diseased somehow, pockmarked by hideous scars. Through the algae and the grime I could see the pale, doomed faces of the sailors staring out at me from the portholes, trapped inside their dark tomb of water and salt.

Then another movement dragged my eyes to

the female figurehead and I realized that she was reaching her hand out for me, reaching it right out of the painting. Her bloodshot eyes were almost popping out of her head, her charred wooden mouth stretched open wide in a ghastly mockery of a smile, and her insanely long fingers came closer and closer and closer…

With a cry of horror, I turned and fled, sprinting all the way back through the empty restaurant, trying my hardest to ignore the shadows sitting at the tables.

I burst out into the corridor and the open cellar door beckoned me silently forwards. I heard the sound of glass on stone and, before my eyes, a single blue witch ball rolled up the final step – it actually rolled *up* the step and out into the corridor to rest gently against my feet. I stared down at it and a picture formed deep in the depths of the glass, showing me the way out, showing me what I must do next.

Ignoring the protesting squawk of the birds, I clutched the fish hook, which felt cool and beautiful against my hot hand, and ran down the cellar steps as fast as I could go.

Chapter Forty-Four

Emma

When the vet told me that Bailey was doing well, it was like the most gigantic weight had lifted from my shoulders.

"He even ate all his breakfast," she told me. "If he carries on like this then you'll probably be able to take him home this afternoon."

I hung up the phone with a huge smile on my face. Bailey was OK. In that moment, nothing else mattered.

I was still smiling even as I wheeled myself across the road to the Waterwitch. I'd go in there, coax Shell out and then take her somewhere to keep her out of Jem's way and cheer her up. Maybe we could drive around the coast, stop off for a cream tea – nice, normal things that I should have done with her from the start rather than taking her to witchcraft museums and medieval guildhalls and magic shops.

Shell hadn't locked the front door and I dragged

it open with some difficulty and wheeled myself over the threshold. Then I noticed the smashed jar of fish hooks, and my good mood instantly evaporated. When I wheeled myself over and saw the drops of blood glistening on the glass I felt my first flash of alarm. I glanced at the big oil painting and it unnerved me as much as it ever had. The dark waves glistened wetly as if they really would be damp to the touch, and it seemed as if the figurehead was staring directly at me with those mad, haunted eyes of hers.

I turned away from the painting and wheeled myself out to the corridor with the monster staircase. The cellar door was closed and it was completely silent out there – and strangely, unnaturally cold. I shivered and ran my hands over my arms. No one had thought to turn the heating off when we'd left yesterday, and a nearby radiator was warm to the touch, but the air was absolutely freezing and my breath actually smoked in front of me as I called Shell's name. There was no reply.

Not knowing what else to do, I hurriedly searched the library and the kitchen and the rest of the downstairs rooms, but there was no sign of her, and she didn't respond to any of my shouts, or pick up when I called her mobile. I decided she must be on the first floor but, as I couldn't get upstairs myself, I had no choice but to call Jem.

Chapter Forty-Five

Jem

The ringing of the mobile sounded like a chainsaw that would split my head in two. I fumbled around on the bedside table, finally snatching it up and pressing the button to stop that deafening noise.

"What?" I croaked out the word while clutching at my head with my free hand.

"I'm at the Waterwitch." It was Emma. "I think you need to come over."

"I can't." The thought of moving from this bed was enough to make me sweat. Every part of my body ached. I couldn't remember ever feeling so ill. I was about to hang up but then Emma was saying something about Shell.

"Slow down," I said, trying to concentrate on her rush of words. "What are you talking about?"

"She ran over here earlier," Emma said again. "She's in the inn somewhere but I can't find her — she must be upstairs. She's hurt herself — there's a broken jar on the floor of the restaurant, and blood on the glass—"

"All right." I was already reaching for my clothes. "Just wait for me there."

I hung up and then got dressed as quickly as I could. I sat on the edge of the bed to tie my shoes but the action made me feel so dizzy that it was several moments before I could stand up at all.

I forced myself down the corridor and out into the street. It wasn't a particularly sunny day but, even so, the light seemed blinding and I had to shield my eyes as I crossed the road.

Emma was waiting for me in the restaurant. "I've looked all round the downstairs rooms," she said, "and I can't find her anywhere. She must be upstairs."

I saw the smashed jar on the floor. The sight of the glistening drops of blood there was enough to clear my head a little.

"I'll go and look for her," I said. "She's probably just in her room. Perhaps she didn't hear you shout."

I hoped with all my heart that was true. Emma followed me out to the staircase and said, "It's *freezing* in here!"

"Is it?" I wiped sweat from my forehead and said, "It feels hot to me. I'll be right back."

Climbing the stairs seemed like the most gigantic effort. My body felt ten times heavier than it normally did, as if I were wearing a diving suit that made every movement painful and slow. The air felt too thin and the stairs seemed to go on and on for ever. I was out of breath by the time I got to the top of them. The sirens and mermaids carved into the wood there seemed to be looking right at me with snarling expressions of dislike that I couldn't remember ever noticing before.

The long wooden corridor stretched unnaturally out in front of me, the stained-glass window of the squid attacking the *Waterwitch* shrinking down to the size of a postage stamp at the far end. I pinched the bridge of my nose, closed my eyes and, when I opened them again, the corridor looked quite normal. It was just the flu making me dizzy.

I called Shell's name, and the act of doing so made my throat hurt, and my jaw ache, and my temples throb. There was no answer so I set off down the corridor, intending to check her bedroom, but as I was walking past Room 22 I heard a thump from within so I threw open the door and walked inside. The door swung closed behind me and, all of a sudden, out of nowhere, I couldn't get my footing on the wooden floorboards. They seemed to lurch beneath me, rising and falling like the deck of a ship tossed about on the swell of stormy waves. I staggered into the wall and had to lean against it to keep from falling over.

In another moment the rocking feeling had passed, although the pain in my head pulsed worse than ever. I looked up and took in the room. Empty. The thump I'd heard must have come from outside. But the buzzing sound in here was louder than I had ever heard it. It sounded like there was a whole swarm of insects trapped somewhere close, desperate to get out.

I left the room and quickly went through the others but Shell was nowhere to be found. With a growing sense of unease, I climbed the steps to check the second floor.

Chapter Forty-Six

Emma

As I waited for Jem, my bad feeling got worse and worse. I could see actual frost, sparkling on the carvings of the monster staircase. It shouldn't be cold like this. It didn't make sense.

Then, all of a sudden, the cellar door creaked slowly open, just like it had the first day I'd arrived. Dark shadows spilled out of it, along with a laugh that hit me like an anchor thrown straight at my face. A single blue witch ball rested in the threshold. Shell was definitely down there. I should have guessed.

Quickly, I wheeled myself to the foot of the monster staircase, taking care not to look at the mixture of teeth and tentacles carved into it, glittering dangerously in their coats of frost, and called at the top of my voice for Jem. There was silence. I shouted up again but still nothing. Perhaps he was on the second floor. I could sit here and wait for him to come back or I could get myself down to that cellar somehow and check on Shell myself. Jem would see my wheelchair when he came down and would know where we were.

I turned away from the staircase and wheeled myself over to the cellar door. The laughter had stopped now, but that just made me feel even more concerned.

"Shell?" I called down the stairs. But, whether she heard me or not, she didn't answer, either.

Every instinct screamed at me to get up out of the chair and run down those steps but running hadn't been a possibility for me for a long time now. Wishing that Bailey was here to help me, I reached around the back of my chair for the walking stick, unfolded it and stood up on legs that already trembled. My spine still hurt from the fall I'd taken yesterday, and the last thing I wanted was to tumble down that stone staircase and crack my head open at the bottom of it. The Waterwitch had had quite enough of my blood and it sure as hell wasn't getting any more, not today, not ever again.

I put my hand on the wall, my cane on the first step, and carefully lowered myself down on to it.

That movement was too much for my back and

it instantly went into spasms. My fingers flexed involuntarily and the cane fell from my grip, rolling away down the stairs. My trembling legs couldn't take my weight any more and I collapsed down on to the step with a jolt that brought tears to my eyes. My hand balled into a fist and I banged it against the wall in frustration, which really didn't achieve anything. Then I let out a string of swear words, which didn't achieve anything much, either.

"You're not getting the better of me," I said, through gritted teeth, and I had no idea whether I was talking to my ruined spine, or my feeble legs, or my tired heart or to the Waterwitch itself. All I knew was that I was getting myself down to that horrible, hateful cellar even if I had to crawl every inch of the way on my hands and knees to do it.

So it began. There weren't all that many steps. In fact there were eleven. I know because each one is seared into my brain. My arms and legs throbbed as I lowered myself down but it was nothing compared to the blinding column of agony that was my spine. At one point I looked back over my shoulder and saw my ugly monster of a wheelchair poised at the top of the stairs and it might as well have been at the top of a mountain. However difficult it was to get down, it would be pretty much impossible for me to get back up. This journey down the staircase would be a one-way trip until someone came to help me.

At last, I was on the final step, and I snatched up my walking stick and pulled myself over to the doorway with the palms of my hands. I saw Shell at once and there was this soft roaring sound in my ears – like listening to the echo of the sea inside a seashell – as all my worst fears were realized right in front of me.

She stood in the centre of the room, surrounded by witch balls, a blue witch bottle at her feet. Gripped in her hand was a monstrous great fish hook, gleaming cold and silver and sharp, with cruel pointed barbs at the end. I could see it reflected back at me in the dozens of witch balls. Shell had the point of the hook pressed against her neck, right beside the jugular. One swipe and she'd have her entire throat ripped out.

"Shell," I said, trying to keep my voice low and steady. "What are you doing?"

"This is … this is what she wants me to do," she replied. "She's here. She's standing over there in the corner of the room."

I gripped my stick in one hand and used the other to press against the wall, finally managing to haul myself upright with an inelegant, lurching movement that left me gasping for breath.

"Jem is looking for you," I said. "I really think you'd better put that fish hook down."

I took a slow, dragging step towards her, but Shell shrieked at me to stay back.

"OK, OK!" I said, my whole body trembling with the effort of standing. "I'll stay right here. I won't move from this spot, I promise."

I wasn't entirely sure I could move, even if I wanted to. I was stuck there, unable to go forwards or back, right in the very same room where we first found the witch bottle and my back had been broken all those years ago. I just had to keep Shell talking, that was all.

"Go away," she said, the hook still trembling in the hand at her throat. She must have pricked the skin because a tiny bead of blood formed at the end of the hook and ran slowly down her neck. "I don't want you here."

"I can't move," I replied. In fact, I couldn't even stay standing. My legs simply wouldn't take the weight any more. I gripped the stick, trying to lower myself down gently, trying to soften the fall, but, of course, the stick slid suddenly out from my grip when I was only halfway down, and there was nothing to prevent me from crashing helplessly in a heap.

I was out of options. Worst case scenario I could try throwing my cane at her. There was a chance that might startle her into dropping the hook she was about to cut her throat with. Obviously, it was a slim chance but slim chances were better than no chances at all.

I was just reaching out towards it, trying to ignore all the little flash-pops of pain that raced up my arm like a line of light bulbs blowing out, when I heard footsteps on the staircase behind me.

Chapter Forty-Seven

Jem

I took in the scene in one glance: Emma sprawled on the floor and Shell with a fish hook pressed against her throat. As soon as I'd seen Emma's abandoned wheelchair at the door I'd known they must be in the cellar and I'd known that couldn't be good.

"I killed Dad," Shell said as soon as she saw me.

"No," I replied, slowly, carefully. "No, you didn't. Dad had a massive heart attack. He drank too much. Shell, you know that."

"I killed him," she repeated, like she hadn't even heard me. "With the birds."

Oh God, those birds again! Always with the birds!

"I'm sorry," she said. "I know it was wrong. But I couldn't let him hurt you."

"You're hurting me now," I gasped. Sweat dripped into my eyes and I wiped it away. "Please put down that hook."

"I can't," Shell said. "It's the witch. She wants me to—"

"There is no witch, Shell," I said. "You're upset still, about what happened to Mum. It's OK to be upset, but it's making you confused and—"

"I AM NOT CONFUSED!"

It was the first time in my life I could ever remember hearing Shell shout. I flinched as my headache intensified, like a hot metal band being slowly tightened around my skull.

"The witch is real," Shell said. "Her name is Cordelia Merrick and she's here, she's right here in this room with us. I don't know why you can't see her but she's standing over there by the fireplace."

"There is no one standing by the fireplace!" I burst out louder than I had intended. The hot band tightened another notch and even my eyeballs seemed to ache, as if they were about to explode in their sockets. "The only people in this room are you, me and Emma."

Chapter Forty-Eight

Shell

I gazed at Cordelia. She wasn't looking at Jem or at Emma, she was only looking at me. Her bloodshot eyes seemed to burn into my skin. She tried to say something but only a gurgle of pain came out as the spikes cut deeper into her shredded tongue. Blood oozed slowly from underneath her metal mask, and dripped softly to the floor. I could feel her watching me and willing me to plunge the fish hook deep into my throat, as far as it would go. *It's the only way*, she seemed to say. *The only way to be free…*

"You'd be better off alone," I said, turning back to Jem. "All I ever do is cause you trouble and make your life complicated. You said it yourself last night."

He groaned. "Oh, God, Shell, please don't throw that back at me now. I didn't—"

"Don't say you didn't mean it!" I cut him off. "We both know that you did!"

"I'm not perfect, OK? But I do love you." Sweat

ran slowly down the side of his face but he didn't seem to notice. "Don't you know that if you died I'd die, too? For God's sake, Shell. Please. Don't leave me here by myself."

I frowned, confused. Suddenly I felt a bit less sure about the fish hook and started to lower it. The witch was getting inside my head and putting dark, desperate thoughts in there. They weren't mine. I was supposed to be fighting them off, not embracing them. She was trying to use my own pain against me.

The birds ruffled their feathers, staring at me expectantly. One of them knocked up against the witch bottle, causing it to roll along the floor.

Cordelia hissed then – a dreadful, hateful sound. And then, to my horror, she lunged at me, dragged the poppet from my pocket and hurled it into the overflowing pump in the corner of the room. The doll landed with a splash and then sank to the bottom beneath the weight of all those nails. With a cold, cruel laugh, the witch turned, raised her arm, and pointed her bloodied fingertip – pointed it right at Jem.

Chapter Forty-Nine
Jem

I couldn't understand what was happening at first. I only knew that I couldn't breathe. My lungs were full of water, and so was my throat, burning with the taste of salt, and then I was on my knees and choking it up on to the floor. But it wasn't just water – there was sand in my mouth, and seaweed, pieces of coral that cut my cheek and broken shells that scratched along my tongue, sea pebbles that lodged in my throat and barnacles that chipped against my teeth. It felt as if I were heaving up the entire contents of the ocean. I tried to breathe and only swallowed more water, my lungs on fire with the effort of trying to draw in air.

I could hear Shell shrieking. "Don't you *dare* touch him!"

I turned my head and saw her feet planted firmly in front of me. Emma was on my other side, her hand gripping my shoulder as I retched. It was only the three of us there in the room.

So how could it be that, beyond Shell, I could suddenly see a fourth person? With my sister blocking the way I could only see their feet, bare upon the stone floor. At first they seemed diseased, ravaged by some terrible skin condition, but then I realized that they were in fact covered in a hard coating of barnacles and limpets, molluscs and zebra mussels, algae and slime. There were even sea sponges growing upon the ankles, and clusters of tube worms creeping up those pale, white legs.

I tried to shout at Shell to get away, but I couldn't speak a single word. An awful spasm wracked my body as I tried to breathe again and more water rushed into my lungs and filled up my windpipe. In that appalling moment I realized I'd been wrong all along, that I'd made the biggest mistake of my entire life, and that I was going to die because of it.

No matter how much water I heaved out on to the floor, there just seemed to be more and more of it. Sand crunched between my teeth and I gagged on thick blades of seaweed that felt like fingers reaching down my throat. Salt made my eyes water and my throat burn and my chest ache. I could hear this awful wet choking sound and knew it was coming from me, and that it wouldn't take too long to die this way.

Shell had been right and I would never get to tell her I was sorry because my heart was beating fast enough to explode in my chest, a creeping blackness blurred the edges of my vision, and there was no room to think of anything at all beyond the pure, blinding agony of drowning.

Chapter Fifty

Shell

I threw down the hook and raced over to the pump, plunging my hand into the filthy water all the way up to the elbow as I desperately felt around for the poppet. The water was too dirty to see anything in the tank but my fingers pressed against something soft and horribly mushy, then ran over something long and smooth and cold, like a tail.

Finally, my hand closed around the poppet and I dragged it out of the water but it didn't seem to make any difference to Jem. Cordelia was still pointing at him and he was still choking up water so I dropped the poppet and snatched up the witch bottle. Yanking out the cork, I spoke Kara's incantation out loud. The birds spread their wings and lifted up at the exact same moment, surrounding the witch, pecking and clawing her.

But it wasn't enough to get her into the bottle. More and more birds burst out from the end of my fingertips until the blood ran down my wrists but it didn't make any difference. Kara had been right – the witch was too strong. She was far, far too strong. My attempt to trap her was only making her angry, only making things worse. Her arm was raised and her hand stretched out through the dark feathers of my birds, still pointing at Jem, still killing him right in front of me.

"NO!" I screamed at her at the top of my voice. "Stop it! It's not him that you want. It's not him that you hate. It's Christian, isn't it? Christian Slade."

The witch's head jerked up at the name. She turned towards me and – finally – I could hear Jem gasping on the floor – tortured breaths that sounded painful and raw, but were breaths none the less. I looked at my birds, still flapping and shrieking around the witch. I might not be strong enough to force her spirit into the bottle, but perhaps an ordinary ghost like Christian Slade would not be quite so difficult.

"Yes," I said. "Christian Slade. I know where he is. I know you can't get to him. But I can get him for you. I can give you what you want."

I said the incantation again but, this time, I substituted "Christian Slade" for "Cordelia

Merrick". The witch shuddered at the sound of his name, the birds lifted away from her and flew up the stairs to Room 7. I felt Christian resist them but his frightened, feeble spirit was no match for them and the birds returned seconds later in a swirl of thrumming, beating wings.

I could see Christian in the middle of them. His dark hair was dishevelled, his eyes were wild, his shattered jaw disfigured his once-handsome face. Old bloodstains marked the white shirt he'd been wearing when the beam fell down to crush his chest on the deck of the *Waterwitch*.

Cordelia flew straight into their midst and threw herself at him. It might almost have looked like a lover's embrace if it weren't for the way I could see her nails digging deeply into the back of his neck, like she wanted to curl her fingers around the smooth white bone of his spine and yank it right out of his body.

I could not see either of them properly, surrounded as they were by birds but soft words seemed to fill the air out of nowhere:

Dearest love of my soul…

Through the black feathers I caught a sudden

glimpse of Christian Slade's terrified, pleading eyes. "Please!" he forced the word out at me through his bleeding mouth. "Don't!"

"I'm sorry," I said. "But it's the only way. And you brought this on yourself."

The voice was there again, the whisper filling the room:

I will hate you until the end of days...

Pecking and clawing, shrieking and flapping, the birds dragged Christian Slade's ghost out of the witch's arms and forced him into the bottle in my hand. Cordelia let out a howl and raced in after him, disappearing into the bottle in a rush of icy air that seemed to freeze the glass. I slammed the cork firmly into the top, put the bottle down and then scooped the limp wet poppet up from the floor. This time, the nails came sliding out easily enough and, when I looked through the torn fabric I saw that the coffin nails were gone and there were just clumps of wet herbs there instead. I shoved the poppet back in my pocket and hurried over to Jem and Emma where they were sprawled on the wet floor, surrounded by shells and coral and thick strands of dark, dripping seaweed.

"Are you OK?" Emma was asking Jem.

"No," he gasped. He groaned and gripped his head with both hands. "God, that buzzing is ... it's going to split my head open!"

As he spoke I saw a squirming water wasp crawl out of his ear and fly away up the chimney.

"It's OK!" I said. "It's just the wasps! They're leaving!"

The first one was quickly followed by others – dozens of them – more than the few I had seen crawl into his ear last night. The witch had probably been sending them since the first day we moved into the Waterwitch.

"They've gone," I said, as the last one flew up the chimney.

"I saw her," Emma said. She'd gone completely pale. "She was really there. She—"

"You didn't look at her face, did you?" I asked sharply.

She shook her head. "No, I couldn't. There was ... it was like a dark mist, hiding her from view. I only saw her feet."

My birds, of course. Protecting us all.

Jem looked up at me. His clothes were soaked with

sea water and there was an anguished expression in his eyes. "I am so sorry," he said hoarsely. "You tried to tell me so many times and I wouldn't believe you."

I threw my arm around him, not caring that he was soaking wet and sticky with salt.

"I don't blame you," I said. "And if we hadn't come here then I might never have realized that the birds were on my side. I might have gone on being afraid of them forever." I drew back. "They did kill Dad, though. They did it because I wanted them to. I was afraid he was going to stab you with that knife. I'm a murderer, Jem."

"It was more like self-defence," he said, and I wondered whether he was trying to convince himself or me. "It wasn't murder. It wasn't."

I wasn't so sure. He was still dead. And white witches did not go around killing people with black magic. This was blood magic now. Killing a human being that way was a dark, dangerous thing to do, the kind of thing that got you noticed by the devil himself... And yet, I would do it again if I had to. I would do worse than that to protect my brother. And that thought frightened me, too.

"You still can't see the birds, can you?" I asked,

looking at the bright, shining eyes that surrounded us.

"I can't see them." Jem touched my arm. "But, Shell, honest to God, I believe that they're there."

I'd been waiting for him to say those words for so long and it was the sweetest feeling. At long last, he wouldn't think I was crazy. I just had to hope he didn't now think I was dangerous instead.

"What are we going to do about the witch bottle?" Emma asked and we all looked round at it, standing innocently on the floor behind us. "Brick it up behind the fireplace again?"

I shook my head. "It will be found there sooner or later and then the witch might be released. There's only one place for that bottle, and that's at the bottom of the sea."

Chapter Fifty-One

Emma

We found a boat to hire that afternoon but there wasn't room for a wheelchair so I couldn't go with them. Shell wouldn't let anyone else carry the witch bottle and was already on board, fidgeting around in agitated impatience.

All of Jem's flu symptoms had gone, just like that. My head was still reeling with everything that had happened down in the cellar. Those awful, unnatural feet. Shell speaking to someone we couldn't see. Jem drowning on dry land right in front of me. It was too much to take in. It was too much to believe. And yet, it was impossible not to believe now, either.

"I'll text you when we get back," Jem said to me.

"Do you think it's safe?" I asked.

"I've taken boats like this out before," he replied. "And the sea is calm enough."

"No," I said. "I wasn't talking about the sea." I hesitated for a moment, then forced out the words,

"I was talking about Shell."

"What do you mean?" Jem asked, but he wouldn't meet my gaze and I was sure he already knew exactly what I meant.

"If she's a real witch — if she has real magic and she can actually kill a man with it, then how can you know for sure she isn't dangerous to you?"

Jem was silent for a long moment. Finally, he looked at me and said, "Shell would never hurt me. I trust her. Let's leave it at that."

"But—"

"Jem, come *on!*" Shell called from the boat. "This bottle needs to be at the bottom of the ocean."

"All right, I'm coming," he called back.

Chapter Fifty-Two

Shell

We sailed out until Looe was a blur on the horizon and there was just a vast expanse of grey ocean all around us. Jem killed the engine and the boat bobbed freely on the waves.

"Ready?" he said.

I nodded and leaned out over the side of the boat, holding the witch bottle above the water. I'd been gripping it so tightly that my fingers seemed glued to the glass and I had to force them open to let it go. The bottle plunged into the sea and I kept my eyes on it for as long as I could as it sank down into the cold, silent world below. Within seconds it was lost from my sight and I stepped back with a sigh.

"It's over," Jem said, touching my arm.

I glanced up at him and tried to smile. "I know."

The witch was gone. She couldn't hurt us any more. My birds took up every inch of available space on the boat – lined up along the railings, perched on the covered roof, scratching around on the deck at our feet. Jem gave my arm a last squeeze and then went to switch the engine back on.

I thought of all that had happened to us recently – recalled that sickening crack when the bone broke inside my arm, remembered all the black bruises and blood, the hauntings and curses and nightmares. As the boat turned in the direction of home, I made a vow that nothing would ever hurt us again. The world was a dark and dangerous place, but I could be dark and dangerous, too, if that's what it took, and if anyone ever crossed me, or threatened Jem, or the life we had together – then they would regret it.

"They'll wish they'd never been born," I said to one of the birds on the nearby railing. It cocked its head, looked right at me with those intelligent dark eyes, and I was sure it understood.

"What did you say?" Jem called over the wind.

"Nothing," I called back. I reached out to stroke the bird's glossy feathers with my bloodstained fingertip. "Nothing at all."

Acknowledgements

Many thanks, as always, to my agent, Carolyn Whitaker. Thanks also to Katie Jennings, Emma Young, Ali Ardington, Emily Hibbs, Jane Harris, Ruth Bennett, Susila Baybars, Jessie Sullivan, Jennifer Cooper and everyone at Stripes for all their hard work on this book, as well as *Frozen Charlotte*.

Looe is one of my favourite places in the world and the idea for the Waterwitch Inn was partly inspired by the incredible Smugglers Cott Restaurant, which was built in 1420 using timber salvaged from the Spanish Armada.

Whilst doing some final research for *The Haunting* I stayed at The Watermark Bed & Breakfast in West Looe where I enjoyed one of the best vegetarian cooked breakfasts I've ever had, and ate too much of the delicious Cornish cream tea. Many thanks to Ash and Debbie for the wonderful hospitality.

Finally, thank you to my family, for their continuous support – and for putting up with all the writing madness.

You'll be sleeping with
the lights on for weeks after
reading a Red Eye.

If you sleep at all...

Get ready to discover more stories
in this bloodcurdling series.

Dare you collect them all?

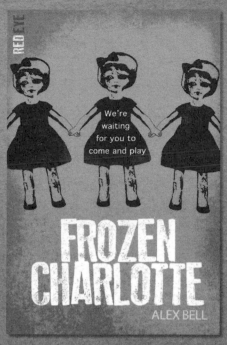

We're waiting for you to come and play

FROZEN CHARLOTTE

ALEX BELL

ISBN: 978-1-84715-453-8

EISBN: 978-1-84715-504-7

Frozen Charlotte

Alex Bell

Following the sudden death of her best friend, Sophie hopes that spending the summer with family on a remote Scottish island will be just what she needs. But the old schoolhouse, with its tragic history, is anything but an escape. History is about to repeat itself. And Sophie is in terrible danger...

eBook available

An extract from
Frozen Charlotte

"Such a dreadful night I never saw,
  The reins I scarce can hold."
  Fair Charlotte shivering faintly said,
  "I am exceedingly cold."

Jay tapped the phone screen to turn it off but,
though the voice stopped singing, the Ouija-board
app wouldn't close. The planchette started spinning
around the board manically.

"Dude, I think that app has broken your
phone," I said.

It was only a joke. I didn't really think there was
anything wrong with the phone that turning it
off and on again wouldn't fix, but then the screen
light started to flicker, and all the lights in the café
flickered with it.

Jay and I looked at each other and I saw the first
glimmer of uncertainty pass over his face.

And then every light in the café went out,

leaving us in total darkness.

There were grumblings and mutterings from the other customers around us and, somewhere in the room, a small child started to cry. We heard the loud crash of something being dropped in the kitchen.

The only light in the room came from the glow of Jay's mobile phone, still on the table between us. I looked at it and saw the planchette fly over to number nine and then start counting down through the numbers. When it got to zero, someone in the café screamed, a high, piercing screech that went on and on.

Cold clammy fingers curled around mine as Jay took my hand in the darkness and squeezed it tight. I could hear chairs scraping on the floor as people stood up, demanding to know what was happening. More children started to cry, and I could hear glasses and things breaking as people tried to move around in the dark and ended up bumping into tables. And above it all was the piercing sound of a woman crying hysterically, as if something really awful was happening to her.

I let go of Jay's hand and twisted round in my seat, straining my eyes into the darkness, desperately trying to make sense of what was happening.

Now that my eyes had adjusted, I could just make out the silhouettes of some of the other people in the café with us – plain black shapes, like shadow puppets dancing on a wall.

But one of them was taller than all the others, impossibly tall, and I realized that whoever it was must be standing on one of the tables. They weren't moving, not at all. Everyone else in the café was moving, even if only turning their heads this way and that, but this person stood completely stock-still. I couldn't even tell if I was looking at their back or their front – they were just staring straight ahead, arms by their sides.

"Do you see that?" I said, but my voice got lost amongst all the others. I stood up and took half a step forwards, staring through the shadows. I could just make out the outline of long hair and a skirt. It was a girl standing on the table in the middle of all this chaos. No one else seemed to have noticed her.

"Jay—" I began, turning back towards him at the exact moment his mobile phone died. The screen light flickered and then went off. At the same time, the café lights came back on. I spun back round to look at the table where the girl had been standing, but there was no one there. The table was empty.

"Did you see her?" I asked Jay.

"See who?"

I stared around for the girl in a skirt, but there was no sign of her.

Anyone would think there'd been an earthquake or something. There was broken china and glass all over the floor of the café, many of the chairs had fallen over and a couple of tables had overturned.

"Who was that screaming?" people were saying.

"What's happened?"

"Is someone hurt?"

"What the hell is going on?"

"Oh my God, someone's been burnt!"

Bill, the owner, had led one of the waitresses out from the kitchen. She must have been the one who'd screamed in the dark. She was still sobbing and it was obvious why – all the way up her right side she was covered in burns. Her hand, arm, shoulder and the right side of her face were completely covered in a mess of red and black bleeding flesh, so charred that it was hard to believe it had once been normal skin. Her hair was still smoking and the smell made me want to gag.

I heard someone on their phone calling an ambulance as other people moved forward, asking what had happened.

"I don't know," Bill said. He'd gone completely white. "I don't know how it happened. When the lights went out, she must have tripped or something. I think... I think she must have fallen against the deep-fat fryer..."

I could feel the blood pounding in my ears and turned back round to Jay. Wordlessly, he held up his mobile phone for me to see. From the top of the screen to the bottom there was a huge crack running all the way down the glass.

"Did you... Did you drop it?" I asked.

But Jay just shook his head.

The ambulance arrived soon after that and took the weeping girl away.

"In all the years this place has been open we've never had an accident like this," I heard Bill say. "Never."

Bill went to the hospital with the girl and the café closed early. Everyone filed away, going out to their cars and driving off. Soon, Jay and I were the only ones left. Normally, he would have cycled home and I would have waited by myself for my mum to pick me up but, today, Jay said he would wait with me, and I was grateful to him for that.

"Thanks," I said. "And thanks for holding my hand when the lights went out."

He gave me a sharp look. "I didn't hold your hand."

A prickly feeling started to creep over my skin. "Yes, you did."

"Sophie, I didn't. You must have… You must have imagined it. It was pretty crazy in there."

I thought of those cold fingers curling around mine and shook my head. "Someone was definitely holding my hand when it went dark," I said. "And if it wasn't you, then who was it?"

Collect the whole series ...

Sleepless
Lou Morgan

The pressure of exams leads Izzy and her friends to take a new study drug they find online. But one by one they succumb to hallucinations, nightmares and psychosis. The only way to survive is to stay awake...

ISBN: 978-1-84715-455-2
EISBN: 978-1-84715-573-3

Flesh and Blood
Simon Cheshire

When Sam hears screams coming from a nearby house, he sets out to investigate. But the secrets hidden behind the locked doors of Bierce Priory are worse than he could ever have imagined. Uncovering the horror is one thing, escaping is another.

ISBN: 978-1-84715-456-9
EISBN: 978-1-84715-574-0

eBooks available

... if you dare

ISBN: 978-1-84715-454-5
EISBN: 978-1-84715-505-4

Bad Bones
Graham Marks

Gabe makes a discovery that could be the answer to all his problems. But taking the Aztec gold disturbs the spirit of an evil Spanish priest hell-bent on revenge. Can Gabe escape the demon he's unleashed?

ISBN: 978-1-84715-457-6
EISBN: 978-1-84715-645-7

Dark Room
Tom Becker

When Darla and her dad move to Saffron Hills, she hopes it'll be a new start. But she stands no chance of fitting in with the image-obsessed crowd at her new school. Then one of her classmates is killed while taking a photo of herself. When more teens die it appears that a serial killer is on the loose – the 'Selfie Slayer'. Can Darla unmask the killer before it's too late?

Do YA Read Me?

Do YA Read Me? is the place to go for the latest buzz in YA books. From author insights to jacket reveals, book reviews to sneak peeks – we've got it covered.

Whether you're into romance or horror, dystopia or geekery, this is the site for you.

doYAreadme.tumblr.com

Follow us on Twitter @doYAreadme